THE
LONDON FLAT

THE IRISH HEART SERIES,
BOOK 2

THE LONDON FLAT

THE IRISH HEART SERIES, BOOK 2

BY JULIET GAUVIN

JULIET GAUVIN ✿ LOS ANGELES

Scaoil do ghreim agus ar aghaidh leat ag eitilt!

CONTENTS

For Rebecca.

THE LONDON FLAT

THE IRISH HEART SERIES, BOOK 2

Prologue: The Other Elizabeth

How was this happening?

"Yes, just there," the photographer instructed, as his assistant moved her an inch to her right. And again.

Elizabeth went reluctantly, feeling like an awkward teenager who'd missed the day on royal etiquette.

The tall, balding man in the dark suit behind the camera continued. "Make haste, Dorren."

The assistant named Dorren closed the distance between Elizabeth and the tiny woman next to her. Another Elizabeth.

Beth smiled nervously at her; Dorren's placement had brought her close enough to feel the woman's blue silk dress. The silver-haired lady smiled up at her kindly. The diamonds on her head caught the light from the elegant chandelier above.

"Lovely, we're there. On three. One . . . two. . . .." Beth turned to the camera. She held her smile, trying not to look disbelieving. "Three." The shutter clicked. "Thank you, Your Majesty."

With a wave of his hand, the photographer instructed Dorren to bring in the next group.

PROLOGUE: IN AFRICA

Connor gazed out at the yellow grasslands as two giraffes wandered onto the field. The sky had turned a light crimson with hints of lavender as the sun began to rise.

He'd left Ireland a month ago. Left Lara. This trip had been as interesting as all the others. The freedom of going from country to country, being known only as the Irishman who cared about the histories and people he met, who appreciated the items they valued—instead of Connor Bannon, *Irish bleedin' noble.*

Here, he needed only a guide and not the security fleet his life sometimes required outside of Dingle.

It was usually a relief to travel the continent, falling into this local legend or that, sometimes finding a piece his European collectors would value, and sometimes walking away with only a grand story to tell.

But now there was Lara.

He'd taken to watching the sunrise and the sunset every day, seeing her lovely face in the sky, in the way the wind swept through the ancient trees, in the way the colors changed.

He'd left Ireland knowing that this trip would be different. He had his own demons to slay. Keanan's blood to battle. And it hadn't been easy—he was still in the middle of it.

Every time he thought about the maggot who'd nearly taken Elizabeth away, the bile rose up and the hatred threatened to consume him. He'd followed her wishes and had him placed in a hospital instead of a prison, but the anger . . . it still lived inside him. Gradually, he learned to work through it. To let his mother's compassion and empathy wash over him. To choose kindness instead of revenge.

Still, he would watch Stephen carefully. And never take Lara's safety for granted again.

She was all that mattered. He'd spent his time thinking about how they'd left things. Wondering if they would ever be on the same page. Wondering if he'd be able to break through that cool wall of hers. The one that kept her just out of reach, hidden away. She'd turned into a different person during their months together, but he knew she saw their relationship as something *other*—an escape from reality, something destined to meet a fateful end.

But Connor thought differently of fate. Ever since that encounter all those years ago . . .

Moving forward, his strategy would be extreme—a gamble. But one he would take. He needed to know. Cutting his trip short was the only way.

He considered his plan again and again. The realities of melding two very different worlds together, of integrating her into his insane life, was a problem for another day.

First, he'd have to break the wall down ... and it wouldn't be pretty.

CHAPTER 1: TUESDAY

"Cheers." Beth nodded to the cashier. Grabbing her strawberries with cream and picking up her shoulder bag, she moved to sit at a table in the outdoor square adjacent to the Covent Garden Market.

It was cool for mid-May in London. A rare spring.

The sun shone without the awful humidity.

She speared a strawberry and popped it into her mouth, delighting in the sweet, tangy blend of flavors. English strawberries were the best. Literally, the best.

She'd never tasted a bad strawberry in England—every single one was at least one hundred times better than any other strawberry she'd ever tasted in her life.

She opened the flap of her bag to extract the photos she'd just developed.

Digital photography had many perks—the instant gratification, the instant feedback, the freedom to play in post—but she found she still liked to hold the memories in her hands.

It had been weeks since she'd developed a new batch.

The first photo was taken at McGann's Pub in Doolin. The small band played at the front of the main room. Smiling faces looked on.

She scanned the rest of the pictures, remembering her month-long trek across Ireland. She'd gone everywhere, visiting pubs, tourist attractions, even hostels. While she no longer felt capable of enjoying a good night's sleep in a room full of bunk beds, she enjoyed dropping in during the evenings.

The most interesting people stayed in hostels. She'd met twenty-somethings from Sweden, thirty-somethings from Australia, and even forty-somethings from Belgium.

Nights were often spent around a fire pit or a dimly lit common area, everyone contributing something to drink, and someone always traveling with a guitar.

There was nothing so wonderful as firelight and the warm sounds of an acoustic guitar with new friends. Those moments always felt endless, like gifts from the Universe. No matter your age, those nights always made you feel sixteen again. The world was full of promise, and life could be anything at all. They were perfect.

Well, almost perfect. There had been one thing missing.

She resumed her examination of the stack of photos, finding one of Connor she'd had printed again. Her latest editing software provided a myriad of digital effects which she'd only just started to explore. The vintage rose-colored effect didn't print well, but Connor was beautiful.

It was a photo she found herself gravitating towards time and again: the black and white photograph of Connor in bed, shirtless. His ripped model physique looked photoshopped. A white sheet came up just below the cut of his hips. One arm was bent behind him to support his head. The other lay at his side, the Celtic cross tattoo on full display.

He had been sleeping. She'd wanted to take the picture with his eyes closed, but at the final moment he'd opened them. The resulting look was primal.

A second later he'd seized her by the waist in one lithe movement, and thrown her down onto the bed.

The memory flushed her cheeks and pulled at something inside of her. Spearing another strawberry, she placed the photographs back into her bag and took a lungful of London air.

"Elizabeth?" a deep male voice said from behind her. The British accent was thick and refined at the same time, typical of the posh London set. "*Elizabeth Lara?*"

Beth turned just as the man reached her side. She looked up into the green-gray eyes and handsome face of Wes Cartwright. His expertly coiffed dark hair came to his ears, his shoulders were broader than she remembered, and his full lips invited admiration. He belonged on a catwalk.

She was stunned to see him.

"Wes?!" She shook her head in disbelief, standing up quickly and flinging her arms around his neck. He swept her up into his arms; her feet dangled several inches above the ground.

They both laughed. She used his arms to steady herself as he set her down.

His simple white T-shirt hugged him well. "What are you doing here?" she blurted out.

He narrowed his eyes. *"Me?* I live here. This is where you last saw me, or have you forgotten?"

As she looked up into his gorgeous face, she remembered how young they'd been.

Twenty-one.

Spending the entire summer traipsing around London, the group of them. They'd been such good friends. But as was so often the case, they'd lost touch.

She tried not to think about how it was all her fault. How she'd allowed the law to wipe all of her meaningful friendships away. The fissure in her chest ached momentarily. Losing her friends was a wound she'd hoped to heal during her time in London ... she just hadn't decided on her approach.

"Yeah, of course." She shook her head, her mouth still open in a wide smile. "I just ... God, it's been almost fifteen years!"

"I know." His eyes searched her face and then moved down her body. "Good God, Liz! You look incredible. The years haven't just been good to you, they've preserved you in a time capsule. What have you been drinking and where can I get some?"

Her eyes mirrored his. "You're one to talk, *Mr. Runway.* You could be on a billboard somewhere."

His eyes flashed with excitement. "What are you doing here?"

Beth opened her mouth to explain, but where would she start? "I'm living here for a while." She kept it vague.

"Well, how long have you been back? And why haven't you rang?" he scolded.

She gave him an apologetic look. "A couple of weeks?" Her mouth turned up into an impish grin and then morphed into a frown. "It's . . . a long story. Just needed a change of sorts. I'd been meaning to look everyone up, but honestly," she considered her words, "I didn't know what to say since I was the one who failed to keep in touch."

His eyebrows drew together in surprise. He examined his beautiful friend. She looked embarrassed. He'd never seen her look embarrassed.

She waited for him to say something, but he just stood there, studying her. She didn't want to imagine what he saw—someone very different from the girl he'd known. He stood there trying to pinpoint the change in her; he wanted to understand.

Her back straightened. "Plus, you know, I've enjoyed rediscovering the city alone," she said, with a blasé bravado she didn't feel.

At that his expression finally shifted. He looked hurt. She remembered him well enough to know he was only acting.

"Just for a bit," she reassured him anyway.

He pursed his lips, trying to stifle a smile. She had changed, and yet she was still the same. Proud, but sensitive to the feelings of others. "Are you about done?" He shook his head, teasing her. "Or should I plan to bump into you in a fortnight?" He turned his body to leave.

She grabbed his arm to stop him. "No, no. This is good."

His features transformed into a bright smile as he sat down opposite her.

They slipped into conversation easily, each giving the other a paragraph-long synopsis of the last fifteen years.

She gave him the brief version. About law school and her career in San Francisco, Mags' death, fleeing to Ireland, coming back to London.

He'd apparently gone to graduate school to continue studying art. He'd curated a few galleries, but found that he didn't like working for other people.

Elizabeth wasn't the least bit shocked to hear it. Wes had always been a free spirit and a bit of a rebel. It was lucky for him that he was independently wealthy.

Apparently, he had been married to a Frenchwoman named Margaux in his late twenties. They'd met in Monaco and had some whirlwind romance. They'd met, married, and divorced within the span of six weeks.

It was *so* Wes.

They'd just been friends that London summer, but they were the type of friends who'd always been attracted to each other.

Always walking the line between flirtation and action. Their natural chemistry would have made it easy to fall into something more.

It was like nothing had changed.

Fifteen years gone in an instant.

They stood to hug each other goodbye.

Confirming their plans for dinner that night, he kissed her on the cheek and was off.

Enlivened by her reconnection with Wes, Beth walked back to her flat feeling twenty-one again.

For a moment she allowed herself to think about what it would be like, if they'd managed to find each other after all this time and do what they hadn't done all those years ago.

She fingered something absently at her neck, feeling the grooves of her tiny Celtic cross pendant.

Her symbol for Connor.

They hadn't spoken since that day outside the cottage when she'd chosen to listen to her inner voice instead of going with him. She'd felt the fissure in her chest rip open, but held firm because she *had* to. To follow him in spite of what she knew to be true would have been tantamount to spitting on the lessons it had taken her a decade to learn.

They'd planned to keep their distance while she traveled in Ireland and he in Africa.

Communication would be spotty at best while he was in the region, anyway. And she'd wanted desperately to live only in the moment without checking messages or connecting with anyone who wasn't directly in her path.

It had been very liberating, but she still felt it. The loss of him.

It surprised her how much she'd felt his absence at times. How he'd gone from a complete stranger to . . . whatever he had become, in such a short period.

He'd left Ireland six weeks ago. According to what he'd told her before leaving, it meant he was due back in Europe soon.

They didn't have any explicit understanding about what would happen when he was back. No actual plan to reconnect—she hadn't been able to think that far ahead. She just knew where the Universe was leading her next, and she trusted that the rest would work out just the way it should.

Now faced with the possibility of seeing him again, a delicious shiver roused her body and made the butterflies dance.

He had a hold over her. A hold the depths of which Elizabeth Lara couldn't bring herself to fully admit.

But she *did* know that even if things with Wes picked up right where they had left off, her past relationship with Connor would prevent her from exploring anything romantic with her old friend. No matter how well he knew her . . . or how much chemistry they shared.

Elizabeth walked down the busy London street, feeling more like a giddy schoolgirl than a grown woman as she evoked the Irishman's gorgeous face.

Connor.

14

The last six weeks had been an exercise in being present. In exploring the world, having fun, and feeling whole. She'd tried to keep thoughts of him safely behind a glass shield so she wouldn't fall into the trap of living in her memories, or create unrealistic expectations about the future. But now, with his return so near, the thoughts and emotions broke through the glass wall and tumbled out at her. Finally allowing herself to remember him fully made the random Tuesday in May feel a little like Christmas morning.

She stopped at a newsstand, nodding pleasantly at the round man with the cabbie hat behind the counter. The sugar from the strawberries and her conversation with Wes had made her thirsty. She smacked her lips as she considered her choices, finally grabbing a large blue water bottle with a red cap. Her eyes found the photography magazines off to the left; an interesting article on infrared pictures caught her attention.

She'd only recently begun thinking about infrared and alternate light photography.

It was then that she caught sight of a very special color. She swallowed and stopped moving abruptly. A pair of familiar eyes stared back at her.

Ice blue.

Her stomach plunged to her feet. Connor was on the cover of one of the tabloids.

There were two photographs. The large one that spanned the page was of him helping a stunning-looking blonde out of a car.

The smaller one took up one of the corners. It showed two people kissing. The blonde had her arms wrapped around Connor's neck. The headline read: *SUPERMODEL REBOUNDS WITH IRISH NOBLE.*

Her hand was suspended an inch from the photography magazine, but her eyes were fixed on the tabloid.

On Connor's face.

What the . . . ?

For a moment Beth heard ringing in her ears. Connor was back?

Supermodel . . . ?

They'd had no understanding, to be sure, *but . . .*

Her fractured thoughts continued until she was suddenly aware of the short newsstand man, his fingers fussing with his cabbie hat. He was looking at her with interest, squinting through his glasses, his lips set in a line.

Her hand moved from the magazine to the tabloid. After paying for her items she began the thirty-minute walk west towards the flat she'd rented in Belgravia.

It was early afternoon.

There were co-workers grabbing a late lunch.

Mothers with young children.

Tourists.

She couldn't see the people or places as they passed. The faces of joy. The faces of curiosity. The faces of delight.

She failed to stop in at her favorite gelato shop on Leicester Square, which she'd always frequented for a scoop of frutti di bosco.

Took no notice of the street artists painted from head to toe in gold or silver, posing unnaturally still as tourists stopped to take selfies.

Almost walked straight into a little boy of about nine who'd taken it upon himself to seize the handle of the fake silver sword of one of the performers, starting a tug-of-war with the human statue.

Her head was full of Connor.

Of the two months they'd spent together.

She didn't know what to think since she hadn't yet read the article, *but the picture* . . .

Briefly, she connected with her surroundings, noticing a bench a few feet away. She felt a pull to sit. To read. To know.

But not fully trusting herself to read it in public, she walked on.

More than once she considered going backwards or forwards to the Underground. To catch the Piccadilly line to the Knightsbridge station and forego the rest of her walk.

But she didn't.

Her feet went by themselves, one in front of the other.

They carried her through Green Park, one of her favorite green spaces in the city. The mature trees and crisscrossing paths reminded her of the New Haven Green.

She walked past the posh houses and expansive embassies that covered the Belgravia neighborhood, until finally she found herself in front of the three-story London flat she'd rented at No. 3 Pembroke Rose.

Along with the other dwellings off of Rose Square, it was a white stucco building with a grand terrace. Typical of Belgravia.

Built in the nineteenth century, No. 3 was a renovated house with a home dance studio on the first floor, the living areas on the second, and the bedrooms on the third.

It was directly opposite Rose Square, a small but lovely park. So small by London standards that you wouldn't even know its name if you didn't happen to see the small plaque by the locked gate.

Beth walked up the steps flanked by two white columns, to the red door with the mail slot painted royal blue.

She was just about to insert her key, when she heard a voice from somewhere nearby.

"Hello!" he called.

Backing away from the door and turning to No. 4 on her right, she saw a man in his early seventies waving at her pleasantly, a kind smile on his face.

He was standing on the landing looking at her through the space between the column and the building.

"Hi," Beth answered, a little surprised.

Her neighbor at No. 4 was an elegant woman named Olivia in her mid-fifties.

"I've just moved in next door. I'm Brian Lockyear," the man quickly explained.

His accent struck her immediately.

Her surprise beat out her manners. "You're American?" It didn't come out sounding like a question.

"Oh, yes," he answered. "from San Francisco, in fact."

Her mouth dropped open at the coincidence. She quickly closed it and remembered herself.

Smiling politely, she said, "I'm Elizabeth Lara. I'm from the Bay as well. It's nice to meet you."

"Well now, I didn't expect my neighbor to be . . . well, a neighbor," he said with a laugh and then abruptly stopped the sound and looked down.

It was awkward.

"Where in the Bay?" he tried again.

"I grew up in Berkeley, but I live in the Marina now." She was purposely vague. The last thing she wanted was to be asked about why she was in London.

"What happened to Olivia?" Beth countered quickly. Be the one to ask the questions, don't be the one to have to provide the answers.

Plus, she really was curious about Olivia; she'd only just seen her two days ago. She'd made no mention of moving. For all Beth knew, this nice old man could have killed her and taken over her house.

Beth blanched at the dark turn her thoughts had taken.

Brian didn't seem to notice. "Oh, she's quite happily installed in my home in San Fran. We swapped houses through an agency for luxury homes." He sounded a little like Mr. Rogers.

"She's there for the next several weeks while I'm here," he finished in that same upbeat tone.

That was surprising. "You must have quite a nice house for her to agree to such an arrangement," she mused, trying not to sound rude.

For a second she surprised herself by how British it sounded.

Olivia was nice enough, but picky. She was from an aristocratic family with money and then she'd married well . . . *twice.*

Most of the buildings on Pembroke Rose were valued at over £10 million.

He smiled, reading between the lines. "I like it."

Her curiosity kept her there on the landing in spite of herself. "Where do you live?" she pried.

"Oh, my house is in Sea Cliff."

She nodded. Yup, that would do it. Sea Cliff was the most expensive neighborhood in San Francisco, with mansions overlooking the Pacific. Properties there often went for more than $15 million.

Her curiosity was sated for the moment. Her new neighbor surprise had temporarily made her forget about the tabloid in her bag. Now she was anxious to get inside.

"Well, it was nice to meet you, Brian." She gave him a nod and a smile before turning her attention to unlocking the door.

"You as well," he called.

Beth imagined she saw a hint of something in his eyes, but the thought quickly disappeared as she stepped into No. 3.

Chapter 2: An Excess of Riches

Beth walked into the foyer, past the wooden floors, mirrors, and ballet barre of the studio and up the white staircase directly opposite the entry.

She reached the second floor and dropped her keys on the long console table, just inside the large square columns that delineated the living area.

The living room, kitchen, and open library corner took up the entire second floor with one bathroom just off the stairs.

Sunshine spilled through the three large windows overlooking Rose Square. The entrance to the terrace was just off to the right.

The modern kitchen took up the left side, with the dining area in front of the window.

A lounging space and TV sat in the middle of the room. The oversized white couches were French country chic and reminded her very much of the cottage. They'd been one of the features that had endeared her to choosing this flat on her very first day of searching.

Sarah, the owner, was a recent divorcée who'd purchased the building at a steal for £8 million three years before.

She'd renovated it to her taste, adding her own personal dance studio and installing several unique features, like the honeycomb white wall next to the kitchen that held hundreds of wine bottles.

Or the reading nook in the right corner that was large enough to be a proper library, if it had walls.

Her cruel husband had cheated on her with three different women. It was quite the scandal and had been heavily reported in the papers.

She was off having an *Eat, Pray, Love* kind of year. At least that was what the very chatty agent with shoulder-length frizzy hair that looked like a bad perm had told her.

Beth was careful not to share too much information with her.

It was all too easy to imagine the gossipy woman bouncing through the place, showing it off to the next tenant.

Telling them how Beth had just up and left her fantastic San Francisco career after losing her great-aunt. And how she'd had a love affair with handsome Connor Bannon. And how the tabloids had felt compelled to report it.

Or how she'd been held at gunpoint by a mentally unstable twenty-something, saving herself and Connor by throwing a knife that severed the tendons in his wrist.

All while standing in her underwear.

She closed the distance to the couch facing the windows, extracted the tabloid, and let her bag drop to the floor loudly.

The pictures assaulted her again, sending a fluttering pain through her stomach. She fell backwards into the couch, feeling like someone had punched her.

The article, if you could call any story in a tabloid an article, talked mostly about the blonde model. Apparently, her name was Sade Cantrell.

She was a popular British model who had exploded onto the scene two years before, after her relationship with heartthrob actor Chase Cove was made public.

They'd been caught checking out of a hotel together, which was a big deal at the time, because he'd just proposed to someone else.

Now Chase had been caught cheating on Sade—just after proposing to her. The new engagement was suddenly off.

But, the article reported, she got to keep the expensive and rare red stone he'd given her for their anniversary *and* she was now "bouncing back nicely with Irish noble Connor Bannon."

They'd been seen going to dinner in Paris over the weekend and later shared a snog. Something in Beth's chest throbbed when she came to the part about the kiss.

Sade was rich, beautiful, and now had Connor too.

An excess of riches.

Beth's eyes examined Connor's face. She let her fingers graze over the picture.

So he was back.

And in Paris.

And had somehow already jumped in with Sade after six weeks on the African continent.

A thought occurred to her. Maybe he'd been back for weeks? She just didn't know.

Beth had returned to Dingle for her last night in Ireland. It was Mona's birthday. She'd had a grand time catching up with her and Kilian.

Just two weeks ago.

They hadn't said anything.

Maybe they didn't know either?

Her heart sank. Maybe they all knew . . .

The fluttering in her stomach turned to burning. Her blood rose to the surface, making her skin look sunburned.

She felt like a fool.

She'd been so careful to remind herself that Fantasyland was a *fantasy* in Ireland. And here she was, fingering the Celtic cross at her neck and strolling down London sidewalks like a silly schoolgirl.

Letting her thoughts wander to a man she'd only allowed herself to spend time with *after* she'd accepted that their love affair would probably be brief.

It was after reading Mags' fourth letter that she'd resolved to let it be whatever it was meant to be.

Well, now she knew what it was meant to be.

Completely.

Over.

Still.

Her limbs suddenly felt very heavy.

And just as she knew now *what* it was meant to be, she knew too that she hadn't escaped unscathed.

She was mad at herself and mad at Connor. The fact that she was mad at Connor only made her angrier with herself.

After all, she'd been clear with him. He'd just listened.

He'd wanted her to come with him to Africa.

She said no.

He'd hint that he wanted her to stay in Ireland.

She made it a point to change the subject.

The damn man had just listened.

Weren't they supposed to be bad at that?

How could he just move on so quickly?

They had no understanding, but . . . there were times it seemed he felt *much more* than he admitted. Had that all just disappeared?

A few weeks on a different continent and *poof!* All gone.

At least she hadn't fallen in love with him. She took comfort in that.

Her thoughts continued in this irrational way for several more minutes. Alternating between pain, feeling the fool, and feeling so angry she wanted Connor to magically appear in front of her so she could kick him in the balls.

Tossing the paper to the floor, she walked to the kitchen. Angrily, she extracted kale and several other veggies from the fridge, throwing them all into the blender with some ice.

She closed the lid and took far more pleasure than was necessary in hitting the buttons, getting some satisfaction from the way the ice crunched loudly.

After pouring her seaweed green smoothie into a pint glass with the words "jolly good" written on it in black script, she opened the door onto the terrace.

Crossing her arms to her chest, she breathed in the now-cool breeze that was making the mature oaks and firs sway gently in the small park.

There was an elderly couple sitting on a bench holding hands inside the square.

They were just sitting, talking, holding hands. The bald man leaned in to kiss his silver-haired wife on the temple. She smiled.

And something inside Elizabeth stirred.

A pang, a longing, a feeling she would push back down again.

Finding out that she'd never been abandoned by her parents had drastically changed her view of the world—had changed the way she looked back on her own childhood, her own history. But some of the scars remained. She hadn't felt like Connor had abandoned her when he'd left for Africa. But the pictures . . . the fact that he'd come back and she didn't even know. She felt the little girl again. Abandoned. She bit back the tears, wanting desperately to eradicate the feeling of being helpless and hurt and angry.

She forced everything she was feeling about Connor away, and shoved it into a box. She wasn't about to be derailed by a man. She'd come too far on her journey to let herself feel broken. There was too much to do, to see, to discover.

And she was in London. A place she knew well; a place that made her feel like she knew *herself* well. It was a safe space. She rewound her thoughts back to before the tabloid. To Wes. To feeling twenty-one again. She zeroed in on that feeling. Holding on to it and allowing it to wash over her. Choosing to think about the possibilities of the life that lay ahead.

At least she wouldn't have to hold back with Wes. She could let *that* relationship be whatever it was meant to be.

But not tonight.

Tonight she would curl up with a book or a movie or edit pictures. She would order in and have a glass of wine.

Let Fantasyland seep completely out of her system. Or force it out.

She went inside to call Wes on the cell she'd purchased since moving back to London. It had been freeing to be without one, but now with her search for Mags' Matthieu, she needed easy access to her email on the go. The private investigator was out searching.

Elizabeth rescheduled her dinner with Wes for Thursday. He'd promised it would be as unexpected as their reunion had been.

Knowing Wes, that could mean anything.

CHAPTER 3: HER PEOPLE

Sitting at the black iron chair and table set on the terrace, Beth stared at the screen of her new Android phone.

After hitting the circular refresh button for the tenth time, she resigned herself to the conclusion that Barry, the private investigator she'd hired, hadn't found anything new.

She scrolled down to his last email, dated Friday, and read it again, hoping to have some detail magically point to where Matthieu could be.

Ms. Lara,

I've ascertained that Matthieu Fleury was indeed a professor of art & art history. He taught at University College London for more than twenty years.

The issue I've run into is that he retired five years ago and did not leave a forwarding address. No one here seems to have any information about where he might be and my contacts at certain government agencies can't seem to pinpoint an address.

This sometimes happens with older persons. They aren't as tied into the grid as we've all grown to be.

I will let you know as soon as I hear anything.

Respectfully,
Barry Lewis

Unusually frustrated by the lack of news, she dropped the phone carelessly on the iron table with a *clack*.

At the outset, understanding the search for Matthieu might take a while—months, even—hadn't bothered her. But that was *yesterday* morning.

Back then she'd been perfectly content with her new surroundings and getting to fall in love with London all over again.

But *today*, she felt impatient for news.

Her phone buzzed once. She snatched it up, swiping to unlock the screen.

Her heart sank a little as she registered what had prompted the notification.

It wasn't an email from Barry. Or anyone else. Not that she was expecting to get an email from . . . *anyone else.*

It was a text from Wes. A picture message. He'd taken a selfie with an over-the-top *Zoolander* model face and the words, *"Can't wait for tomorrow, gorgeous."*

Always the flirt. Her heart lifted a degree and her lips twitched up into a smile.

The picture made her remember that summer, the feeling of it, the friends. Besides Wes and herself, there were five in the group. Audre Bright, Loryn Davi, and Mark

Stansfield rounded out their odd little club of passionate personalities.

Loryn was the pretty blonde. The demure fashion diva with a good heart. She'd introduced Beth to the super-lux brands *and* London's back-alley street fashion. Although she was one of the nicest people Elizabeth would meet, she was capable of a withering stare any Brit would be proud of, and had that British way of simultaneously giving a compliment and throwing judgment down to an art. *Blue is such a terribly lovely color on you, darling, but this plain black you're wearing is also . . . something.* It was impossible to be angry at her for it, because she was only ever interested in helping.

Mark was extremely good with numbers and random facts. He always made any conversation that much more interesting. Like the time they all watched *Star Wars* together and he told them that France was still executing people with a guillotine when the first *Star Wars* film came out. Or when they'd gone stargazing in the countryside and he'd informed them that it rains diamonds on Saturn and Jupiter.

Wes was the most free-spirited. And the one with the most money to burn. His apartment had been their base of operations. Whether they played pool or went up to his hot tub on the roof, Wes' place usually figured into their plans. He was always up for anything and challenged them all to be the same way. The night could end anywhere with Wes. And it often did. It was part of the reason being near him was so electrifying.

Audre was the ballbuster of the group. No bullshit, big personality. She was fun, but they all knew not to ask a question they didn't *really* want to know the answer to. Beth had described her to Mags once: *She's got these eyes that will cut you down when you deserve it and make you believe that anything is possible when you need it. She's straight up good people.* Mags had nodded understanding instantly, as Mags was wont to do.

Elizabeth sighed, remembering. It was strange to think about them after all this time and feel like it all could have happened just yesterday. How was that possible? It seemed she'd been experiencing that a lot lately. The familiar feeling of stepping back in time, which turned into a sinking feeling once her heart reconnected to her brain and she realized just how much time had come and gone.

Her thoughts stayed firmly on her friends. Where were they all living now? Had they all changed, or were they much the same, like Wes?

Deciding to do some PI work of her own, she grabbed her laptop and settled on the ivory couch to find Audre first.

Next to Wes, she and Audre had been the closest. Beth had thought of her often over the last fifteen years, always with some regret.

A Google search yielded immediate results. Apparently, Audre was a lead curator with the Natural History Museum.

She wrote down the number and then quickly, without allowing herself to think about what she would say or how awkward it might be, she tapped in the number.

Now that the line was ringing, her thoughts turned to the words that would actually come out of her mouth.

Would she even be able to get ahold of her like this? Was it rude to call her at work? What should she say? *Hey, I'm back in London and just looked you up . . . how have you been?*

"Hello, Natural History Museum, how may I direct your call?" a monotone, but cheerful female voice asked.

"Uh . . . yes, hi. I'd like to speak with Audre Bright, please?"

Without missing a beat, the receptionist said, "One moment."

The line was ringing again.

It rang five times and then went to voice mail. Elizabeth recognized Audre's voice. It sounded a little older, but otherwise it was the same.

She wondered if Audre would think the same thing about her, or if she no longer resembled her twenty-one-year-old self at all.

Probably the latter.

Beep.

"Hi Audre! This is probably going to seem like the most random thing ever. . . ." Her voice sounded high to her ears, like she was trying to sound younger, so she cleared her throat in an effort to sound more normal. "So yeah, this is Elizabeth Lara from fifteen years ago here in London . . . with Wes, Loryn, and Mark?"

She took a breath. "Anyway, I know it's been a while, but I'm back in London and I'd love to catch up. I actually

35

ran into Wes by accident yesterday and it got me thinking about everyone. So . . . give me a call when you get this. And sorry to call at work. I found your contact info by Googling you, so yeah . . . congrats on the curator gig! OK, this is a really long message and I'm going to stop rambling now. Hope to talk to you soon. Bye."

She almost hung up without leaving her number, but remembered in time. Anxiety colored her voice as she scrambled to leave her contact information, including an email address just in case it was more convenient.

Just in case she wanted to decline her invitation to catch up without an awkward phone call.

She pressed the red "end" button and let all of the air out of her lungs. Immediately, she sunk back into the ivory couch. After re-filling her lungs with a few cleansing breaths, she settled back into her body.

It was unnerving how much courage that had taken. Like jumping out of a plane you didn't even know you were on.

She felt lighter, though. Like she'd just taken action on something that had been on her to-do list for fifteen years. Which, of course, it had.

It never sat well with her that she'd lost touch with virtually every close friend she'd ever had. And she especially felt the loss of her international friends.

The idea of reconnecting with Audre was exciting in an entirely different way. Like the first day of school or the day before a big trip.

Beth had been close to Loryn, but she and Audre were best friends that summer.

The five of them had met at The Elephant's Crown pub in Bloomsbury. It was a small watering hole that attracted students and grumpy old men alike.

With two archways in the middle of the floor, moss green walls, low lighting and dark wood everywhere, it was exactly the type of English pub Beth had pictured in her head before moving to London.

The wood tables and booths were covered in carved graffiti dating back at least a hundred years, with new carvings continuously being added by patrons.

There were only ten people there at the time, which was perfect because it was already ten at night and it was the twelfth pub she'd visited. She was looking for the right pub, with the right number of people.

Loryn and Audre were there together and so were Mark and Wes. The two sets were sitting at separate booths along the wall when Beth had come in alone.

She'd marched up to the bar and declared, "Barkeep? A round for everyone please."

The room had gone completely silent. Ten pairs of eyes looked at her like she was mad. For buying the round or for using the word barkeep, she couldn't be sure.

It was her third night in London and she'd specifically budgeted for this experience. For some reason, she'd had it stuck in her head that this was something she had to do or she would regret it. Walk into a pub, buy everyone a drink, and then go around and introduce herself.

She knew the Brits would think she was a crazy American, which was just fine by her, so long as they accepted the drink and conversation.

Secretly she'd also hoped to find some kindred spirits. The other Yalies in the program were all friendly, but she could tell it would take some time for them to be themselves with each other.

Beth liked people with whom she could just jump in. Be friends instantly without all the boring getting-to-know-you parts.

She found that treating virtual strangers with an air of familiarity from the start usually worked wonders.

Maybe it was the stress of moving to a different country, or feeling overwhelmed by all the new in their lives, but Beth's tactics hadn't worked on her classmates like she'd hoped. By the end of that summer the Yale in London group were all great friends, but it had taken a while.

After everyone in the pub had their drinks in hand, Beth made her way to the two older gentleman sitting at a corner table by the large window. They seemed like the toughest nuts to crack. They were. She gave up after five minutes of asking questions meant to inspire conversation. They answered in as few words as possible, politely thanking her for the drink, but then growing tight-lipped when she'd tried to find out anything else. A question about how long they'd been friends had been answered quickly and succinctly, in the dry British way. "Oh, probably longer than you've been alive."

She'd moved over to the ladies in their fifties sitting at a table near the bar, who were kind and interested in her life, but very polite. Next was the couple at the back of the pub. They were friendly, but Beth had clearly crashed their evening. She'd spent a few minutes being polite and wishing them well before finally coming to the twenty-somethings who would become *her people*.

"What should we call you, gorgeous?" Wes had opened with as a greeting. "Barmy? Brazen? Or beguiling?" He wiggled his eyebrows for effect.

Audre had joined in. "Any woman who can walk into a pub as cheeky as that is someone I'd like to know." She then turned towards the bar. "*Barkeep?*" She threw Beth a teasing smile before continuing, "I'd like to buy this girl a drink."

Beth knew she'd found what she was looking for. The two sets of friends turned to each other. Introductions all around. They put three small tables together to facilitate the conversation better.

Two hours later, Wes had gotten them all into a trendy club in Soho. The rest was history.

Her phone suddenly vibrated in her hand, bringing her attention back to the present.

It was a London number she didn't recognize. She sat up and hit the green button without thinking. "Hello?"

"Bitch!" Audre half-yelled into the phone. "Where have you *been?*" A little deeper, a little older, but it was most definitely Audre.

Beth let out a sigh. Relief washed over her as she fell back against the couch. She knew then that it would be easy to jump back in with her. To get back to being friends.

They talked easily, openly. It was like coming back for sophomore year of college. Everyone had changed a little, but everything was familiar.

Their conversation was brief because Audre had a meeting about an approaching exhibition.

She was free for lunch, though, and invited Beth to join her at Le Pain Quotidien, the rustic-chic Belgian café in South Kensington close to the museum.

Uplifted by the reconnection and feeling twenty-one again, she went inside to shower and get ready. Briefly she wondered whether that would be the theme of her time in London: *feeling twenty-one again.*

She could sense it.

Another piece of her former self returning, and she was grateful. Nothing and no one was going to stop her from reclaiming herself, fully.

She had a second chance at a new life. And she had every intention of seizing it.

CHAPTER 4: THE RECKONING

By one Beth was seated at a table outside Le Pain.

It was sunny, but a light breeze picked up every once in a while, caressing her bare legs and calling out the goose bumps.

She'd dressed in a fitted blue skirt, white tank top, and black ballet flats.

An awning surrounded the corner café, setting off the white exterior and custom windows that extended down to the fat baseboards.

She sipped her Earl Grey served in LPQ's signature red bowl with no handles. The warmth spread through her fingers, comforting her as she tried not to think about what came next. It had been a friendly and brief phone conversation, but she remembered Audre well enough to know that everything wasn't suddenly OK. There were things to say and her friend would surely say all of them.

Audre came around the corner just then wearing a chic white sleeveless designer dress. Her long wavy hair was as Beth had remembered it—always a little out of control. They used to call it Carrie Bradshaw hair.

Today it was a bright auburn.

Beth's face erupted into a huge smile, which was answered with equal enthusiasm.

She stood as Audre closed the distance.

For a moment they just stared, eyes full of unspoken memories. Searching through the past, searching through the history written in the other's face, trying to fill in the blanks. Then, without saying a word, they threw their arms around one another.

It was several seconds before they let go.

Beth's eyes prickled with tears. She swallowed them back down as she returned to her seat.

Audre rested her arms on the ornate metal chair and took a deep breath, her shoulders rising and falling. She was a little emotional as well. Which was saying something since Audre didn't *do* heavy emotions.

"Hiya, Babes," Audre breathed, shaking her head with a disbelieving smile. Several thoughts crossed her face.

Beth thought she caught disbelief, confusion, anger, and finally a frustrated sort of happy.

Beth bit her tongue; she could sense something was about to boil over. She braced for it. Audre's eyebrows pinched together, her mouth set in a line.

It was coming.

Until finally. . . . "What the *hell*, Liz?!" she practically shouted.

Several people seated nearby turned to look at them.

"Where have you *been*?!" She threw her hands up in exasperation. "Phone calls, emails, I came to California, it was great, and then," she snapped her fingers, "just like that, *nothing*. You went to law school and dropped off the face of the bloody Earth!"

Beth sat back and looked at the table, feeling heartily ashamed of herself. "I know, I know, I know!" She brought her eyes back to Audre. "I'm sorry." She tried to imbue her words with raw honesty. "By that third year of law school I was this soulless robot assassin. I didn't talk to *anyone* on the outside."

Audre crossed her arms and waited for more.

"Seriously, I haven't talked to my suitemates from college, any of my friends from high school. Running into Wes yesterday was the first time I've had a real conversation with anyone from my past in like . . . a decade."

Audre pursed her lips, weighing her words, but remaining unmoved.

Beth stared back, willing her to see how sorry she was. Audre didn't budge.

Finally, Beth threw up her hands and said what they were both thinking. "I suck. OK?" Some part of her younger self broke through, with the bold honesty she used to pride herself on. "I *totally* suck."

There was no use in sugar-coating it or explaining it all away.

Audre's lips almost twitched. A glint of amusement colored her blue eyes.

"Yes, you *do* suck." She nodded, her face unchanging. Beth's lips twitched up at hearing Audre's very proper British voice say the word *suck*.

"I suck." Beth nodded like there was no arguing the point. "I am the suckiest friend ever." She bit the inside of her lip to keep from smiling.

"Yes," Audre titled her head, "you are."

Her face finally broke; the measured mask gave way to the piercing inquisitor. She sat forward and the onslaught began. "Why didn't you at least respond to my emails or calls with . . . I don't know, something . . . *anything*?" Her West Yorkshire accent made it sound like *sumthin . . . anithin*?

Audre's eyes turned skyward. She was remembering. "The smallest message would have been enough. 'Hi . . . *I'm alive*. How are you?' You just completely ignored me like a right foul *git*!"

"Total git." Beth nodded, knowing Audre was only pausing to take a breath.

"I mean, honestly. Who *does* that? I thought we were such good mates and then you just dumped me!" Audre's voice was starting to lose some of its bite. She was starting to sound genuinely hurt now.

For the first time, Beth considered how it must have felt to send emails and phone calls out into the world, which were never returned.

It was sickening. Thoroughly and completely. It took coming face-to-face with Audre for Elizabeth to realize what she had done to her friend.

Feeling the weight of it, she collapsed inwards a degree, and the shame rose up again with a new intensity. She shook her head, her voice low and sad. "I dumped my life, Dree."

There was no escaping the consequences, the choices she'd made. She'd opted out of her life and now she had to deal with the damage she'd done. Elizabeth had prided herself in never taking a false step in her career, with each case, each opponent. The thought that she had made one giant mistake after another in her personal life made her chest feel tight and her heart hurt.

After a pause, she bit the inside of her lip. "I dumped my life," she repeated, trying to get her friend to understand that it wasn't about her.

Audre said nothing.

When Beth finally looked up, her friend's face had softened with compassion and that same look Mags had given her in the hospital . . . *pity*.

Elizabeth shrugged. With heartbreaking truth and tears that threatened to brim over, she said, "I lost a decade."

It was a simple truth she'd already come to terms with. But it was the sort of truth that continued to crush her again and again, each time unlocking some new level of understanding.

Audre finally spoke. "I want to keep having at you and say that it's all a load of rubbish, but you just look too bloody sad."

Audre's eyes scrutinized Beth; she narrowed in on something. "So what changed? What snapped you out of it?" She leaned forward, clasping her hands together.

The waitress made an untimely appearance just then, asking to take their order.

She hadn't gotten two words out before Audre jumped in. "Oh, bugger off! Can't you see we're in the middle of something!" She waved the woman away impatiently.

Then, she took a deep, frustrated breath and called after her. "Apologies, Sarah! I haven't seen my friend here in fifteen years and I'm a bit barmy at the moment."

The young twenty-something waitress with short brown hair scurried off, looking back to nod as Audre apologized.

Beth gave her a worried look. Audre quickly waved it off with a roll of her eyes. "Oh, they're used to it; they know me here. Know I'm a bit cheeky, but they love me anyway because I tip like I really am barmy. She'll be chuffed, I'm sure."

Turning back to Beth, she said, "So? What happened, Luv?"

Beth winced at the endearment, incapable of divorcing the word from her memories.

Connor.

She forced the memories away and focused on the question. For some way to give her the abbreviated version. But there really wasn't an easy way to gloss over everything. Especially with Audre; she would see what Beth wasn't saying.

Almost instantly, her body crumpled forward. Her tears spilled over, and she shrugged slowly. "I lost Mags."

She bit her lip to keep from crying, but the tears flowed anyway.

"Oh, *Hun*." Audre leaned forward to take her hand.

She hadn't had this conversation with anyone who actually knew her before. A fresh wave of pain hit.

For the next ten minutes Audre listened to Beth explain about becoming an attorney and losing her life. About what it had done to her, what it had turned her into, what it had cost. And about Mags passing and leaving her the seventeen letters.

She described how she'd dropped everything to vacate her life. Dumping the optometrist John, whom she'd been dating for a year.

Moving to Ireland. Reading the letters. Rekindling her love of photography. And so on.

She talked about the friends she'd made in Dingle without mentioning her brief love affair.

Her time on the road visiting the rest of Ireland.

How she'd slowly started to reclaim bits of herself. How she'd come back to life.

She'd only left out Connor and the revelation about her parents. Mostly because it felt too heavy and complicated to go into on top of everything else.

By the time she was finished, she felt exhausted.

It was like confessing to a priest . . . or a shrink.

They sat in silence for a minute.

"You really stopped taking pictures all those years?" Audre said with genuine surprise and no bite. Gravity colored her words. Like this bit, more than any other, made her understand the true degree to which Beth had abandoned her life. Had become a completely different person.

Beth nodded, equally surprised that of all that she had revealed, her friend had honed in on the one piece.

Audre could see the question on her face. "It's just that you were always taking photos. You never went anywhere without a camera."

Beth shook her head and shrugged. "Just to take snapshots. It was nothing by then. I was really focused on photography when I was younger. By the time you met me, I only took group photos and tourist shots."

Audre raised an eyebrow, "Uh, no, Babes. You may have taken some group shots of all of us, but you were taking artistic photographs even then."

Beth had to think about that. She'd only displayed the group shots on her walls.

The rest of the photographs were in several boxes under her bed. It had been a while since she'd looked at them.

Again, Audre could read her like a book. Impatiently she added, "The pint glass with all of our reflections in it? The picture of Loryn's eyes through her hair? The time you made us all break into Kensington Gardens after hours so we could climb and pose with the Peter Pan statue using only torches from Wes' flat to light the scene?"

Oh yeah. The memory of each picture came rushing back. Beth broke into a smile. "Yeah, I remember now. We almost got caught, but we outran the guards." She shook her head and sat back in her chair, feeling it all again. "I was so relieved we made it out of there. Didn't want to get blamed for getting you all arrested."

Audre waved a hand. "Please. Even if they'd caught us, we wouldn't have been carted off. Wes would have talked them down."

That was probably true. Either with his silver tongue or his connections. Wes wasn't just independently wealthy— he had ties to the royals.

They'd never pressed him about it, but the more time they'd spent with him, the more obvious it became.

Still feeling the weight of her confession, Beth was eager to focus on something outside of herself. To fill in the gaps of her friend's life. She'd missed so much. "What about you, Dree?"

Audre considered her for another long moment. Considered whether she should allow her friend to steer the conversation away from herself. She read the pleading in Elizabeth's eyes. Read the pain.

"Oh, well, let's see." She softened, providing the escape she knew her friend needed. "Finished at Oxford with my degree in History of Art, worked as a cataloger at various small places, went back for my D.Phil. at Oxford. Worked as a restorer at the Louvre for a couple of years—"

"Wow." Beth couldn't help cutting in.

Audre's eyes sparkled. "Yeah, it was pretty fantastic. The best part was getting to walk around at night." She shrugged. "You know, long hours."

For the first time in a long time, the nerd in her wanted to say *cool*. "What was *that* like?" Beth asked with wide eyes.

"Beautiful . . . eerie . . . magic." Audre looked off into the distance as she remembered.

Her words lingered in the air, giving Beth chills. She could picture it. *The Louvre at night*.

After a long moment, Audre continued. "Then I came back to London, worked my way to curatorial assistant in prints and drawings, and finally was named curator of digital media."

"What does that mean?"

Audre launched into her work description spiel. The one every professional had ready in their back pocket when asked to explain what they did for a living.

"I preserve, maintain, collect, and archive digital assets. I also oversee the creation of new digital works such as creating digital images of paintings or drawings; sometimes I have short films made about an artist or a piece. I'm kind of a jack-of-all-trades."

Even though it was rehearsed, Beth could see how much Audre enjoyed her job. "You love it." It wasn't a question.

Audre almost swooned. "Oh yeah. Curator in digital media is still a fairly new concept, so not every museum has one. I get loaned out to the British Museum, the National Gallery sometimes; it's great. No day is the same."

"So is that your secret?" Beth asked.

"Secret to what?"

"To staying . . . *you*."

"How do you mean?"

"Well, I completely lost myself in my job. Became a different person. But you—you seem the same. You did everything you wanted to do, but stayed the same," Beth observed.

"I suppose I just get wrapped up in it. It doesn't feel like work to me. Cliché, I know."

Talking about her job made Audre practically glow. It seemed to feed her, not suck her soul from her body.

Beth tucked that away for later. "So did you keep in touch with anyone from that summer?"

"I talk to Loryn all the time. She finished at UCL, turned her love of fashion into her job. She's a buyer for Topshop. Mark did something in finance and then went mad. Had some nervous breakdown, took all of his money and bought an island somewhere to live off the grid. I don't know." Audre rolled her eyes.

"And Wes I haven't seen in a few years. Although he did work as a restorer under me when I was a curatorial assistant. That lasted a whole week, if you can believe it." She laughed.

"He was always late and was so bored with the work, it was clear to the both of us that he had no business working for someone else . . . or as a restorer."

"Yeah, he might have mentioned as much. Not that you worked together, but that working for other people didn't suit."

They exchanged knowing smiles.

Yup, *so* Wes.

Then Audre's lips twitched up. "How'd he look?"

Beth gave her a short laugh. "Like he belonged on a billboard."

Audre smiled wickedly. "Did he ask you out? I bet he asked you out. You two were always so . . . *something*. The most surprising thing about that summer was that you two *didn't* shag."

Beth turned the color of her drinking bowl.

Audre gave her a look of total exasperation. "Please. You had so much chemistry. How you managed to keep your clothes on? Beyond me. Now I, I would have just got on with it. I bet he's a *fantastic* shag." She bit her lip and let her eyes float up, picturing it.

Beth held up her hands, in a *calm the bloody hell down* sort of gesture. "He didn't ask me out. We're just going to dinner to catch up. Like you and I are doing right now."

"Uh-huh." She narrowed her eyes and then remembered something. "You were always *total* crap at knowing when someone fancied you."

Audre looked around and waved Sarah back to the table, even though they hadn't yet gotten around to opening their menus.

"What are you doing? I don't know what I want yet." Beth quickly reached for the menu, but her friend seized it before she could open it.

Audre gave her a knowing look. "I don't have forever, Babes. Only half an hour to eat, if that, and you would surely squander it all trying to decide what to order. I'll save you the trouble. You'll love it, trust me."

Beth held out her hands in surrender. She didn't take forever, did she?

She sat back in her chair. "I forgot how bossy you can be."

"Eh . . . excuse me? How many times did you put your taste buds in my hands?"

"A few," Beth admitted reluctantly. She'd found very quickly that Audre was an excellent orderer. She had a real knack for understanding what people liked.

"And how many times did my talents fail you?"

"Zero."

"OK, then. Sarah, my friend here will have the Chorizo and Potato Frittata and I'll have the Butternut Squash and Feta Frittata."

"To drink?" Sarah asked politely.

"Two Bucks Fizz," Audre answered automatically.

"What are those?" Beth asked as Sarah left to put in their orders.

"Fresh orange juice topped with organic Prosecco."

"Sooo," Beth thought out loud, "a mimosa?"

"Yes, but doesn't Bucks Fizz sound more fun?" Audre mused. "Where were we? Oh yes, we were talking about Wes."

She leaned forward and positioned herself in a very serious manner, like she was Diane Sawyer and the next words from her lips would be the million-dollar question. "Do you think you'll snog on your date?"

She said it seriously, but all Beth could hear was Audre's voice crescendoing like a teenager broadcasting, "*Beth and Wes sitting in a tree K-I-S-S-I-N-G.*"

Beth threw her napkin at her, then answered in a rush of words. "I don't know. When I saw him it was like nothing had changed, so . . . maybe? I'm kind of conflicted. There was someone in Ireland. It's over now. *Very* over. But, I don't know, I'm not as over it as I'd like to be before moving on with someone else."

That was an understatement.

Audre didn't miss a beat. "Was he hot?" She really hadn't changed at all.

She bit her lip, trying not to think about the specifics. "Yes."

Audre looked confused. "Then why is it over?" As if that was all there was to making a relationship work.

Quickly, without thinking too closely about it, she said, "He's moved on with someone else." She said it like she was talking about someone else. A friend of a friend. She needed the distance.

"Oh." Audre paused, thinking. "Well, was it serious?"

Again, she had to think about it superficially; she couldn't let the emotions stick to her, "Yes and no. I thought it was more serious for him than me." She waved a hand, almost like she was trying to swat away her feelings.

"Then what makes you think he's moved on?" Audre shook her head and narrowed her eyes. She was fresh on the trail of something. She could see that Beth was holding back. A lot.

Elizabeth didn't want to have this conversation. She felt like Audre was closing in on her. Or forcing her into a corner where she'd have to confront her feelings. No escape.

The sound of rustling paper distracted her. She turned towards the table to her right, next to the window.

Her face fell. The woman had just opened the tabloid, Connor's blue eyes stared back at her. The kissing photo slapped her again, and the box into which she'd forced all of her emotions on the subject rattled loudly. The glass wall she'd built threatened to shatter in an instant. She winced.

Audre followed her line of sight, looking from her face to the paper and back again.

Beth closed her mouth and turned back to Audre, trying to look calm.

Audre's eyes returned to the paper. Beth could hear the cogs turning in her head.

"Nooo!" Audre finally put it together. *Loudly.*

Beth stared daggers at her.

She lowered her voice conspiratorially. "You mean the guy you dated was *Connor Bannon?*" She looked shocked . . . and impressed.

"I don't want to talk about it," Beth said through tight lips.

"Oh, Babes, he's like beyond hot." Audre sat back in the chair and breathed, "What I wouldn't give to ride *that* stallion." She said it more to herself than Beth. Then she sat forward. "And he's titled. Did you know?"

Beth wanted to sink into the ground and disappear. "It may have come up."

"He's a notorious bachelor. Women have been trying to land him for *years.*"

All the color drained from her face. "Well, I wasn't trying to land him. We just . . . spent time together. He went to Africa for six weeks—or however long." She shook her head, correcting herself as she remembered that she didn't even know how long he'd actually been gone.

It was like she'd completely misread him. Didn't know him at all.

Beth's voice was careful, measured. "We had no understanding, no plans for after he came back. So . . . *it's fine.*" She said the last two words in a hard tone. "I just thought of him from time to time. And now I just have to get used to *not* thinking about him." She looked into her friend's face. "That's *all.*"

Audre got over the shock of it and could now see Elizabeth's pain...and pride.

"Well, you're better off!" Audre threw up her hands like she was expelling the sad energy that had just made its way to their table before continuing, "He's a tosser—and you know what's the best medicine?"

Beth tilted her head, already knowing what she was going to say. "Let me guess. Snogging Wes?" she said in a British accent.

Audre shook her head. "No, Babes. *Shagging* Wes."

Audre looked so certain, it made Beth smile. Some of the color returned to her face.

Their food and drinks arrived just then. Sarah arranged their plates and then scurried away again.

Elizabeth was grateful when Audre dropped the Connor talk. They both began to eat eagerly, letting the food and mimosas work their magic.

Elizabeth felt better. "What about you, Dree? Are you seeing anyone?"

"Oh, you know me. I need variety. No one has been able to hold my interest for very long. They're all professionals around here. They just get more and more . . . what's that word? *Zombiefied.*

"I want to meet someone who has the balls to do exactly what he wants to do in life. And not because he has family money so he can, but because he can't or won't give up on that thing that makes him feel alive. Is that too much to ask?"

"Sounds like you need a young twenty-something artist." Beth took a sip of her Bucks Fizz. The bubbles tickled her nose.

"Er . . . been there, done that. *Twice*." She looked up and to the side. "Wait . . . no, *thrice*." She took a bite of her frittata. "They're always so *needy*." She scrunched up her nose. like her former young artist lovers were more a nuisance than anything.

Beth was tired of talking about men. "So how's work, then?"

"It's fine." Audre sighed, letting her shoulders fall forward as she remembered. "We had a major crisis with an exhibition we're having next week—that's the meeting I went to this morning. It's a mess and, no, I don't want to talk about it. How's the photography going?" She volleyed back.

Finally, a subject that didn't weigh her down. "It's great. I've been having so much fun using my new gear, learning the cameras, the editing software. It feels amazing to have a camera back in my hands."

"What have you been shooting then?"

Beth finished her bite of frittata. "Everything really. Landscapes, people..." she remembered Fungie, "...animals."

"Oh yeah?" Audre's interest piqued, "What sort of animals?"

"Well, I got this pretty unbelievable shot of Fungie the Dingle Dolphin and a great white in the distance." Beth

58

shivered as she remembered the experience. She hadn't thought about it since it happened two weeks before.

Audre's eyes widened. "A great white in Irish waters? Documented? *Bloody fantastic*!"

"Oh, I'm fine, thanks though," Beth reassured her friend playfully. Touched at her lack of concern.

"Wait, I thought you said you left Dingle six weeks ago."

"I did. But I went back for a friend's birthday. During the day I went to swim with Fungie and then in the evening I went to my friend Mona's party. It was my last night in Ireland."

"This was what? Two weeks ago?"

"Yeah…" Beth narrowed her eyes. "How'd you know?"

"There were reports. It was a big deal; it's never happened before." She took a bite of her food, then sat back in her chair. Thinking.

After a quiet moment passed between them, Audre swallowed and sat forward, eyes wide. "Do you think I could take a look at it?"

The question caught Beth mid-chew. She finished her food and then answered, "OK."

Beth was pleased with the picture, but didn't like to think about it. "I haven't edited it yet or anything, but I have the RAW file on my tablet."

She extracted the tablet and found what she was looking for. Seeing it again made her hands shake. It was a pretty shot, but it wasn't fun to relive the memory.

Audre's eyes grew even wider as she looked at the picture. Her hand came to her mouth, and for several moments she didn't say anything.

She was completely stunned.

The picture showed Fungie several feet away, facing her. Rays of sunshine broke through the water, lighting the dolphin perfectly. In the distance was the great white, also lit by rays that had broken through the clouds and through the surface of the water.

"How did you manage to take this?" Audre whispered, her voice reverent.

"I bought underwater housing for my Canon 5d Mark III? Exposed for—"

"No, no, not the technical specs. How did you not go completely mental? Jesus, if I had seen that coming at me I would have got the hell out of there."

Elizabeth turned red. Not because she was embarrassed, but because it was the closest she'd ever come to dying.

And she hadn't even known it at the time.

"I was focused on the dolphin." The blood fell to her feet as she remembered. "My brain registered the second object, but I didn't really see it. I didn't even know anything was wrong when Fungie started to swim circles around me— I thought he was just being playful.

"Then he put his nose to my feet and forced me to straighten my legs so he could propel me back to the boat." Her entire body shook at the memory.

"I didn't see how large the object was until I was out. Fungie sped away and the great white turned in the opposite direction once I was on the boat. I swear my blood curdled, Dree.

"At first I didn't really believe what I was seeing. Then I zoomed all the way in on the picture." She shook her head. "My friend, Kilian, who took me out on his boat—well, *Connor's* boat, but Kilian operates it—saw the picture over my shoulder and then we just kind of froze as we watched it swim away from us."

Her voice grew low, quiet. "There were various reports of the sighting by the time we got back to shore. We were both pretty shaken."

Beth had read that marine biologists had found the shark and tagged it, so they would know if it ever came back into Irish waters. Which was a relief, because she wasn't sure she could ever swim with Fungie again after that.

If she ever got to swim with Fungie again. Was she even allowed to swim with him again? He was Connor's. . . .

She focused her attention back on Audre, who had zoomed all the way in on the picture and was looking at every inch. "Wow, it's a great photo, Liz. May I send it to myself? I'd like it for my wall."

"Sure." Beth shrugged. "But remember, I haven't had the stomach to work on it yet, so it's far from perfect."

"Rubbish." She rolled her eyes. Then she looked up, amused. "I'm glad you didn't die, Babes."

Beth laughed nervously, in spite of herself. "That makes two of us."

CHAPTER 5: MISSED YOU

Beth opened her eyes to the glare of the screen. Her laptop sat open on the bed next to her. She squinted at the time and looked around the room.

It was almost nine on Thursday morning. She'd been up late editing pictures, lost in each memory, each new set of characters and places.

It was becoming more second-nature to her. Opening a picture and instantly seeing what needed to be done to draw out the image, draw out the story.

The last time her droopy eyes had registered was 4:00 a.m.

After her long lunch with Audre, Beth had walked around with her camera, following her curiosity. Every turn, every decision was guided by some internal compass, some need to witness and observe and record what was around the next corner.

The last finished image was still on the screen. It was a photo of the elderly couple she'd seen in Rose Square the day before.

London was beautiful any time of the year, but the spring was one of Beth's favorite times to be in the city. She was both weary and invigorated from the photo walk. Her phone's pedometer told her she'd covered almost twelve miles.

Ready to get off her feet, brew a cup of tea, and have the scone she'd just picked up in Soho from Gail's Artisan Bakery, she was just about to walk up the steps of No. 3 when she turned back towards the square. The couple had their eyes closed. The man had his cheek against her hair; the woman leaned into his side. A look of sheer contentment colored both of their faces.

She'd quietly approached the gate and taken a photo of the moment. Most of the picture was of the black iron gate to the square and a bundle of overgrown orange-red bell-shaped flowers that hung a couple of inches from the gate.

The couple was framed by the hanging bell flowers. They were slightly out of focus, as Beth had intended, their intimate embrace only recorded as an impression.

She lay back against the bed, imagining what they had been feeling. Imagining what that would be like. To grow old with someone.

She extended her arm without moving, using her fingers to find her phone. She grasped it and brought it to her face.

Nothing from the PI.

She was about to check the weather when she noticed the envelope on the top left corner. A text.

It was probably Wes. Without hesitating, she tapped the screen to open it.

The words made her sit bolt upright. Her heart in her throat.

Hello Miss Lara, I'm back on the continent! Hope to see you soon. -Connor.

There was a second message.

P.S. I've missed you.

Her heart pounded in her ears, making her head throb. She took short, shallow breaths.

"Seriously?!" she shouted.

How did he even have her number? It was two weeks old and she'd only given it to Barry, Wes, and now Audre.

I've missed you?!

What the hell was he playing at?

Thoroughly disgusted and rattled, she spiked the phone into the thick blue comforter with a thud.

Angrily, she flung herself from the white four-poster bed, holding on to one of the square columns to propel herself onto the light wood floor.

She walked past the two large windows that faced the square, into the massive walk-in closet where she grabbed her black yoga gear and threw it on the chair.

The en suite was just past the closet. She quickly brushed her teeth, put her hair into a ponytail, and changed.

The dark rose yoga mat was right where she'd left it downstairs in the studio. She couldn't stop to think, or the frustration, the anger, the disgust would swallow her.

65

She unlocked the gate to the square and set the mat out in the middle of the fluffy green grass behind the bench and walking path, under a fifty-foot London plane tree.

She didn't even bother taking her shoes off. Immediately, she threw herself into one of her routines. Warrior, to tree, to plank, to upward dog, to downward dog, to child's pose with a few variations thrown in.

She moved through the sequence quickly, going faster and faster as she went. She could feel the thoughts, the feelings coming for her. She had to outrun them. Had to keep going.

They almost had her.

Before she knew what she was doing, she took off at a sprint, going through the gate and down the block, cutting through several back alleys, catching a walk sign across S. Carriage Drive, and crossing into Hyde Park.

Beth wasn't a runner. She didn't like it; she didn't ever do it, for fun or for exercise. But she ran through the winding pathways of Hyde Park like her life depended on it.

With every stride, she reached a little further, pushed a little harder, willing her body to overwhelm her brain. *Demanding* her body override her brain.

When she had nothing left in her lungs or her legs, she stopped. Looking around, she took in the grove of trees that surrounded her. She was alone.

Alone in the world.

No one left.

No longer able to keep it inside, she threw her head back and screamed with her entire body, shaking with the force of it.

She screamed because she was alone; she screamed because she'd lost Mags; she screamed because she'd abandoned her friends; she screamed because she'd read Connor so completely wrong.

With an answering crash of thunder, the skies opened. The water came down and mixed with her tears.

She closed her eyes and welcomed the flood.

Standing completely still, she let the rain wash over her.

In a matter of seconds Beth was soaked to the bone.

Twenty minutes later, the rain was still coming down and she was a sopping mess.

The run and subsequent release were cathartic, but they'd left her drained to the core.

She walked up the path to No. 3 with some effort. She didn't see him until she was on the steps.

Brian was holding her yoga mat. "I just thought I'd bring this back to you. I was returning from my walk when I noticed you leave it . . . and then the rain," he explained.

"Thank you." She nodded, stone-faced, because she was incapable of anything else.

She'd left it all out in the grove.

"Is everything OK, sweetie?" He was examining her. "No bad news, I hope?"

"No, no." Her voice was weak. "Thank you, I'm fine. I've just been going through a mid-life crisis—or whatever thirty-five-year-olds have." She shrugged.

In that moment she was incapable of sugar-coating the truth, even for this stranger.

She looked up into his eyes. "Do you have family back in SF, Brian?"

His eyes softened. There it was again, that look of pity. "No, my wife passed some years ago and my daughter. . . . No, I don't, Elizabeth. I have many good friends, though." Beth didn't catch the flash of pain in his eyes.

"That's good. Friends are important," she answered in the same soft, vacant tone.

She was still standing in the rain on the steps just outside the cover of the landing.

"Yeah, I alienated all of my friends. Every single one of them. I don't know what happened—I just . . . lost a decade." She shrugged mindlessly again and motioned with her hands in a *poof, it's gone* gesture.

He appraised her with shrewd eyes. "But you're here. Trying. Aren't you?" His voice was encouraging; he sounded more and more like Mr. Rogers.

She walked up the steps and crossed to the door. Turning, she said, "Yes, Brian, I suppose I am. Because that's all you can do, right? Try?"

He nodded kindly, handing her the mat.

He opened his black umbrella and walked back to No. 4.

Beth showered and went back to bed. When she woke several hours later, she felt lighter. Better able to embrace what was in front of her.

She was trying now.

She could feel guilty about the past, but it wouldn't help mend her friendships; it wouldn't help her feel less alone in the world.

It would just continue to weigh her down. So she picked herself up and marched downstairs for a late lunch.

She was in her favorite city. She'd reconnected with two old friends. She had a camera in her hands and enough time and money to figure out the rest.

Seeing that the rain had stopped, she threw open the terrace doors and listened to the birds chirping happily in the trees of Rose Square while she ate her omelet.

She had a lot to be grateful for.

Brian's demeanor had reminded her so much of Mr. Rogers that something she'd once heard him say played on a loop in her brain: *"Often when you think you're at the end of something, you're at the beginning of something else."*

She was most definitely at the beginning of many things.

And with Wes in charge of tonight, it was sure to be an adventure.

Still feeling a little homesick for Mags, she walked the length of the living room to the honeycomb wall with the wine. She'd stored the blue box with the red ribbon in one of the empty spaces.

She took it back to the library nook in the corner and sat on the window seat, curling her feet underneath her.

She was on letter twelve. She'd "read" letters eight, nine, ten, and eleven on the road in Ireland. Mags' messages had become increasingly unpredictable.

Letter eight was a list of her favorite quotes.

Letter nine a list of her favorite books.

Letter ten was another SD card, this time filled with old pictures Mags had digitized. They were mostly of Beth's mother. Pictures of Beth and Carolina together.

One where Carolina is holding her as a baby, Beth's fat cheek smashed against her mother's. Another of her mother crouching behind her, arms extended as Beth tried to walk by herself.

Others of Beth, Carolina, and Mags together. There were even some photos of Carolina and Mags in France. One was a group picture with Carolina, Mags, another young woman with brown hair, and two men, one younger, one older.

Beth wondered if one of the men was Matthieu. She wished Mags had thought to leave her the names of the people in the picture.

Those photos meant so much. She had spent a lot of time going through them, and she'd printed a few so that she could run her hands over the faces. She gazed at Carolina now with compassion and love. Mags had managed to return her mother to her even in death.

Letter eleven was a list of recipes Mags knew Beth loved. That letter had moved her to tears again. She thought about how it must have been for her, knowing she was dying, keeping it a secret, and simultaneously planning the letters—deciding what she'd leave behind.

The recipes were a testament to how well Magdalen knew her. She hadn't even realized she regretted not asking her for them until her aunt had delivered them to her from the great beyond.

She extracted letter twelve from the box, examining the yellow envelope with her fingers. She opened it to find a single piece of paper with Mags' elegant writing on it.

Dear Lizzie,

When I was younger, I found myself lost in the woods. I don't mean this figuratively; I mean literally lost in the damn woods. I was training for some marathon or other and was too busy looking at my watch, trying to time myself, that I missed the path. Thinking I knew where I was, I cut through the woods in an attempt to get back on track.

I was mad at myself for losing focus, when a beautiful blue butterfly landed on my thumb. Its wings opened and closed, but it stayed perched on my hand, even as I moved to sit on a fallen tree.

I don't know how much time passed, but I was entranced. Completely captivated by this weightless beauty. Even now I can close my eyes and see it like it was yesterday.

Now I'm not going to say that the butterfly flew away and I magically found the path again just moments later. I didn't. The butterfly filled me with awe, and I've thought about that experience many times over the last fifty years, but I still wandered around for another hour before I found my way again.

The point, Lizzie, is not that I got lost, or that I got found, for that matter. It's that getting lost afforded me the opportunity to meet the blue butterfly and carry it with me all these years.

I hope that, wherever you are on your journey, you'll remember that everything happens for a reason. I've found that when you go with the flow and let the wind carry you where it may, the most wondrous things can happen.

Even when that wind comes from a hurricane.

Love You Lizzie,
Mags

Beth clutched the paper to her heart and smiled. She could see it. Mags lost in the woods, cursing the whole time. The blue butterfly.

Let the wind carry you where it may. . . .

Just then her phone buzzed. Her heart dropped to her knees for an instant. She swiped the screen to find a text from Wes. She let out a breath.

Sending something over. You'll need it for tonight. -Wes

Highly suspicious. Briefly, she wondered if he was sending over a parachute because he was taking her night skydiving. Or perhaps a pair of ice skates or riding boots.

As if on cue, the doorbell rang. She went downstairs to find two young women on her doorstep. One carried a big box and the other carried two black, professional-looking makeup cases.

They walked past her into the foyer, without ceremony.

"Hi, I'm Elizabeth, can I help you?" She wasn't sure what was happening.

"Mr. Cartwright sent us. Now, if you'll just direct us to where you'd like to get ready, Miss." The woman with brown eyes and a very bright, very unnatural shade of short red hair waited for further instruction.

The other girl was shorter, with light brown hair and bright blue eyeliner.

The red-haired woman radiated impatience. "My name is Althea, and this is Carly. Now where would you like to get ready, Miss?"

OK. She was clearly a no-nonsense kind of gal.

"Upstairs." Beth led the way to the en suite off the master.

Over the course of the next two hours, Beth asked the pair if they knew where Wes was taking her. They didn't.

She tried to make small talk, but it appeared they had no interest in talking at all and answered only with the fewest words possible. So she sat back and let them do whatever they were there to do.

They didn't ask her what she wanted or what she liked; they just jumped in and immediately started creating a very specific look.

By the end, Beth was standing in front of the full-length mirror in a long cream sleeveless v-neck satin gown with intricate beading on the bodice. It was a classic mid-twenties silhouette. There was no defined waist; instead, the fabric gathered at her mid-thighs and then flowed outward slightly.

Her hair had been curled from top to bottom and then pinned along part of her forehead, giving the illusion of bangs. The rest of her brown hair was gathered in an elegant updo just below her right ear. A beaded hair band separated the bangs from the rest of her hair, like a crown.

It was very *Downton Abbey*.

The doorbell rang again. Althea and Carly had just finished packing. "We'll show ourselves out."

Beth thanked them with a huge smile. She could have sworn Althea looked almost pleased by the gesture.

With one last look she packed the beaded clutch that came with her ensemble and headed down.

Wes was in the foyer at the foot of the stairs. He was wearing a tuxedo with a white vest and a bow tie. The tuxedo jacket had tails. It was *incredibly Downton Abbey*.

His mouth dropped as he watched her coming down the stairs.

She stopped halfway down and put a hand to her head like she was fluffing her hair. A pose for his benefit.

He was most amused.

"So are we going to a super-exclusive speakeasy?" Beth's eyes were wide; she was now completely excited for the night.

He brought his thumb to trace his lower lip, considering her. "Something like that."

She reached him and they kissed once on each cheek. He lingered on the second kiss.

"You look stunning," he said at her ear.

She invited the butterflies that came with his compliment. "Thank you." She smiled back. "You look quite dapper yourself."

A charged moment passed between them. She could feel the heat start to rise to her face, so she broke the silence. "You were quite thorough in picking out this outfit. How'd you even know my shoe size?" She looked down at the character shoes that matched her dress.

"It's all up here." He tapped a finger to his temple.

She shook her head and narrowed her eyes. "How?"

"Well, I do believe there was a rather unfortunate incident where I picked you up when I was completely sloshed and dropped you." His face was contrite. "I ruined your new shoes, remember? The heel broke and you twisted your ankle?"

She'd nearly forgotten the incident, but now she remembered the lovely pair of black boots with the interesting and oh-so-comfortable oval heels.

"*Right.*" She nodded. "I was so angry with you, I made you buy me a new pair."

"Yes, but it wasn't enough that I pay for them; you said, 'If I have to lose time doing this, then so do you.'" He repeated her words in an American accent, then looked at her with genuine affection. "You were livid. It was so endearing."

Beth looked down. He'd never been that direct. His flirtation had always been light, fun. This was something else.

He tipped her chin up so he could see her. "You used me as a crutch that entire weekend."

She remembered. "That's right. My ankle was swollen so I could only walk a couple of blocks, which meant I was stuck with Pizza Express and the small movie theatre for entertainment those two days."

"Well, Pizza Express was your favorite, so no real loss there," he chided.

"True," she allowed, remembering her addiction to the upscale pizza restaurant.

With a slow smile, she added, "But you stayed with me and missed that big football match you were looking forward to."

He shrugged carelessly. "Eh," he said, but then fixed his smoldering eyes on her. "I'll take being your crutch any day of the week and some holidays as well."

His smile was sweet, honest.

It made Beth's insides flutter.

For the first time in a long time, she felt nervous.

And so she took Mags' advice for the umpteenth time and let the wind carry her where it may.

Chapter 6: Back Alleys by Candlelight

Wes' private car dropped them off on Ensign Street.

"Are we in the East End?" Beth asked as Wes reached behind him to take her hand.

"Yes, we're in Tower Hamlets."

She trailed two steps behind. "When are you going to tell me where we're going?"

He didn't turn around to answer. "Patience, we're nearly there."

He led her down a dark alley behind a black gate, until they reached an elliptical arch that framed two old wooden doors. The walls on either side of the building were covered in peeling rose-colored paint.

It looked like something you would find in a back alley in Rome, not London.

A big, bald, burly man in head-to-toe black stood just outside the doors. He held his hands clasped in front of him and wore an expression of stone.

Beth could just make out an earpiece.

Wes nodded and the man instantly opened the door for them.

They stepped inside the very old building. The walls were made of deteriorating brick, the floors of stone. A thin string of track lights illuminated the walls at regular intervals.

There was no one in sight.

Wes led her down a hallway on the right, past the ancient-looking staircase, and finally through a door.

He held the door open for Beth with his body, watching her closely as she stepped inside.

Her jaw dropped; the scene took her breath away.

Sufficiently pleased with her reaction, he gave her a wicked smirk. "Welcome to the BC Club."

"As in 'before . . . Christ'?" She didn't know what to say.

Wes chuckled. "As in 'by candlelight.' It's a secret pop-up club that's for members only. Tonight our host is Wilton's Music Hall."

A waiter walked by carrying a tray of fresh drinks. Wes grabbed two and handed one to her.

The rectangular hall reeked of history. The floors were thin, wooden, and worn in. The walls were made of stone and peeling paint. The ceilings were tall; a balcony, supported by thin spiral columns, looked over the main floor. A huge elliptical arch framed the stage where a live seven-piece orchestra played 1920s jazz.

Tall round tables with long white linen cloths stood around the space. About two hundred people—women in flapper dresses or *Downton Abbey* gowns, and men wearing tuxedos—spoke animatedly to each other over cocktail glasses while some danced on the floor.

The entire space was lit with thousands of candles and a few chandeliers that had been rigged from the barrel-vaulted ceiling for a little extra light.

"Pop-ups have become trendy in London and there's some element of secrecy to them, but not like the BC Club. Membership is limited to two hundred and you can't simply buy your way in."

"So what you're saying is that there's no Facebook group you can sign up for to get tickets," she joked.

"Most certainly not!" he said with mock snobbery.

She took a sip from her champagne coupe. "Is this . . . ?"

"Cristal?" he finished for her. He shrugged absently. "Of course."

Of course.

"There are other drinks at the bar if you want to try a Sidecar or Gin Rickey." Wes nodded a greeting to a group of men standing near the bar in the back.

They tipped their heads and smiled.

"Aren't you going to introduce me?" she asked, looking towards the men and playfully jabbing his ribs.

"I would but it would be an exercise in futility."

She wondered if she should be insulted.

He gave her a short laugh as he registered the look on her face. "No, it's just that we use assumed names even if we know each other outside of the club. We pretend to be other people, which is usually a gas."

He steered her farther into the room. "However," he continued, "tonight's about catching up with *you* and having some fun, so it's not bloody likely I'm going to share you with that lot."

Her eyes brightened with humor. "So every time you come to one of these, you choose a different name? A different backstory?"

He nodded, amused by her amusement.

"Yes, but I'd actually like to get caught up on Elizabeth Lara, not some fictional character you create."

Beth pursed her lips; she'd been a little too eager to become someone else for the night. "How about a compromise?"

"I'm all ears." Wes took a sip of his champagne.

"How about . . . we keep our actual histories, but change our names?"

"In that case, I'll be Arthur," he offered.

She scrunched her nose. "Isn't that your middle name?"

He narrowed his eyes like he'd been caught, but was somehow pleased that she'd remembered. "Yes."

"Fine, you can be . . . *Art.*"

His forehead creased; she could tell he found the nickname distasteful.

"OK, how about . . . Count?" she suggested, eagerly awaiting his reaction.

He raised an eyebrow. "As in Dracula?"

"Duke?" she offered, thoroughly enjoying the dramatic looks of disbelief and dislike on Wes' face as they emerged one after the other.

"Come on, not even Duke? I bet there are actual dukes in this room; it's not that far-fetched." She looked around, still teasing. And then some of her amusement dissipated as she realized just how *many* royals were in the hall.

Some she recognized outright; others just had that aristocratic air about them. "I'm right, aren't I?"

He looked around and nodded in various directions. "There's one, there's one over there. Under that arch there are two—or at least they will be when their fathers die. . . ."

He smiled wide, playing along with her. "Art it is."

Then the smile faded a degree, and his eyes grew intense. He brought his hand up to her face; a finger brushed her cheek. "And who will you be tonight?"

She turned pink, then she thought about the name she wanted to use and recovered. "I'll be . . . *Natasha.*" Her eyes flashed as she said it.

He laughed.

An admiring warmth touched his eyes. "Natasha," he repeated with a little bow of his head, his eyes fixed on her face. He took her hand. "Pleasure." He kissed it, letting his lips linger on her skin.

She bit the inside of her lip to keep from laughing.

Wes finally finished kissing her hand with a loud *smooch* sound, and the wicked grin returned. "Let's go up to the balcony; we can sit and talk . . . maybe feed each other strawberries, if you're amenable."

He didn't wait for her to respond. They made their way up to a small table overlooking the dancing couples. A waiter quickly attended them, but with no menus to look through, Beth deferred to Wes.

Or Natasha to Art.

He ordered filet mignon for the two of them. A bottle of Cristal and, after giving her a long look, a plate of strawberries.

"Tell me . . . *Natasha*," his tongue wrapped around the name, "what brought you back to London?"

She shrugged. "I told you. I just needed a change."

He tilted his head and frowned. "Please, I know you better than that. Why London?"

She shook her head. "I was really happy here once. Can't that be enough?" She clasped her hands in front of her on the table.

Wes was light, fun. She didn't want to bring the conversation down by divulging all the complicated details of tracking Matthieu down . . . or talking about her parents.

He reached over and pried her hands open, taking one in his.

With an intensity, a maturity she'd never seen before, he said, "You can tell me, Liz. Why did you quit California and turn your life inside out?"

She bit her lip, thinking through it. He looked so concerned, so genuinely interested in the hurricane that had brought her here.

Beth took a breath, leaned forward, and told him about Mags' death, about the letters she'd left behind. About having kept some secret for thirty-five years. She told him about the guilt, the month-long hibernation. The people who'd helped bring her back to life. She mentioned having a short-lived romance in Ireland, but didn't mention Connor's name.

Beth told him about Mags' Elsa and how she'd asked her to find Matthieu. About finding out about what really happened to her mother, and finding out that her father wasn't her father.

It was a surprise how easy it was to explain it all to him. She didn't feel heavy or sad, like she thought she would.

Except when she described how she'd completely changed. How she was no longer the vibrant person he knew. She liked how he remembered her and didn't want his opinion of her to change.

She admitted that she used her clients and the law to subconsciously get back at her parents.

Describing the awful, boring person she'd become was the most difficult part. She couldn't get through it without visibly cringing.

But then she described falling in love with photography again and the decision she'd made not to go back to San Francisco.

She told him about traveling across Ireland. About the beautiful nights with strangers and guitars. And living only for the present moment.

By the time she was finished, she found that it was a great relief. Now he knew. Now he could see all of her.

He listened patiently through it all, squeezing her hand here and there when he could tell it was difficult for her to continue.

She waited for him to have some sort of reaction.

"Well?" she prodded impatiently. "I've just, you know, laid it all out there. Say something."

His eyebrows drew together, his expression measured.

For a moment, she thought he was disappointed in her. Disappointed for changing. Or maybe those were her insecurities talking.

Finally, his face broke into a smile. "You? A bore for ten years? I can scarcely believe it."

She let out the breath she didn't know she was holding.

Leave it to Wes.

"Well, believe it." She took a sip of champagne. "Until three and a half months ago, my entire existence was dominated by this little thing called the law and I was a vicious, vicious human being."

He brought his thumb to his lip. "Oh, I don't know. I bet any chap would be chuffed to be tortured by you."

She shook her head and smiled. "I wasn't that kind of lawyer."

It was like going to confession, *again*. She looked down at the table. "OK, so now you know that I was basically . . . *not me*."

"You seem embarrassed to be telling me this. Like you cocked up your life and dropped a clanger just now."

She narrowed her eyes. "Usually I don't need the translation, but 'dropped the clanger'?"

"Admitting something that is enormously embarrassing."

"Oh." She nodded. She didn't know what to say to that. She was embarrassed, but she wasn't used to him calling her out on it.

"You didn't mess up your life, Liz. You got caught up by it. Got caught up in being the best. Now *that* is the Liz I remember." He smiled.

She looked into his face, seeing all the affection and sincerity in his features.

She liked the way she looked through his eyes. It was intoxicating.

His broad shoulders collapsed inwards as he leaned forward.

He held her in his magnetic gaze.

Feeling the familiar pull, she wanted to forget everything else. Forget about recent events. Forget about all the reasons why she shouldn't and just lean across the table and kiss him. To fall in. She'd started to lean forward, mirroring his movement, caught up in the moment, until her brain cut in. She had questions.

"So what about your love life?" she said abruptly, breaking him out of the movement.

Sitting squarely back in his chair, he replied, "What would you like to know?" He kept her hand.

"Why is there no one in your life? I told you about the romance I had in Ireland and about the man I was with for a year." It was his turn.

He shook his head and frowned. "There's nothing to tell. The women here, they're all the same. I don't believe I've had anything longer than a month."

"Because they're all the same?"

"Because I need more than a pretty face. A real connection. That . . . pull you feel to someone. A sense of excitement. Nerves, even."

"You mean someone that gives you butterflies." It wasn't a question.

"Well, I wouldn't have put it quite like that, but yes." His green-gray eyes smoldered. "Butterflies, Elizabeth."

She nodded, understanding, falling into the spell he was casting with his eyes.

"I'm looking for something more extraordinary. And I'd like to think I know the difference."

His words were smooth and seductive, but something irked her. She'd heard this particular explanation before.

"So you just lead women on even though you know they won't be able to hold your attention?" Her voice was full of censure.

He heard the reproof and judgment in her tone. "No, not at all. I'm completely honest from the start. I tell them it's just physical, just temporary companionship. Most women understand and appreciate my candor. And, of course, there are those who say they understand, but really expect that after a couple of weeks with them I'd grow to feel differently."

"Oh."

"Yes, *oh*. I'll thank you not to judge me." His back straightened, and he squeezed her hand in a playful reproach.

She shook her head, lying, "I wasn't judging."

He tilted his head and gave her his *oh, come on* look, or whatever the British equivalent was.

"If I can refrain from judging you for staying with someone for a year even though you didn't love the poor sod, then you can surely refrain from judging me for not going through this life as a monk because love is rare."

Some part of her subconscious recognized that she'd had this conversation before with another gorgeous man in another country.

"So then what happened with Margaux? Why'd that relationship fall apart?" She was determined to understand him.

A sad, melancholy smile transformed his features. He let go of her hand as the waiter returned with their food.

When the man left, Wes answered as simply as he could. "She was French." He shrugged. "Passionate, beautiful, but, as it happens, not particularly predisposed to commitment."

He cut a piece of his steak.

Seeing his sadness, Beth was hurt for her friend, and a little angry. "What? She just left you?"

He finished chewing before answering. "No, I left her after I found her in bed with two other men. I wasn't too keen on sharing."

He laughed, remembering.

Huh. "You seem . . . strangely OK with it. Not angry at all." She squinted, trying to really see through him.

"Why should I be? I knew that she was . . . *hot-blooded*. She even admitted to me before we got married that she'd never been faithful to any man. I believed that I'd be the one to change that."

He looked down at his plate. "But you can't change a person. It isn't within your power." He took another bite.

Beth cut into her food, struck by how Zen he was about it.

"I'll tell you what, though. I don't regret it for a moment. I loved her. I married her. I learned something about life, about myself."

He brought the fork halfway to his mouth, which brought Beth's attention to his lips.

With an intensity that made her insides squirm, he continued, "It taught me to know what I want in a life partner. A friend who gives you butterflies. Someone who is beautiful, strong, kind, steadfast. Someone who can keep up with me, who has an adventurous spirit."

All the blood rose to her face. "That's quite a list." She looked away towards the people dancing below.

She noticed for the first time that, either because of the candles or the peeling yellow paint, the entire place shimmered with a golden light that gave it a dream-like quality.

"Have I made you feel uncomfortable?" he asked.

She turned back to him; he probably wasn't even talking about her. They'd always flirted. She felt silly now for thinking he could mean her. "Not at all." She smiled, recovering.

Her tone was considerably lighter. "So, Cartwright, how do you spend your time these days?" She forked the piece of meat she'd just cut.

He looked taken aback, almost confused by the turn the conversation had taken. He'd thought he was making progress with her. Now she wanted to talk about business?

"Er . . . OK . . . I started a charity focused on the arts. You remember I told you that I did some curatorial work?"

"Yes, and then Audre also mentioned you worked as a restorer under her," Beth added.

He looked surprised. "You saw Audre?"

She nodded. "Yesterday."

"Yes, I did. I worked as a restorer for about a week—did she tell you that as well?" He looked amused.

Beth returned the look.

He ran his fingers through his hair. "Yes, I suppose I was a total cock-up of an employee." He laughed.

"The point is," he resumed his story, "that I wanted to do something different, not just follow the curator route and end up the head of some collection. I wanted to take my love of art, for putting together collections, and bring something new to the world."

He looked invigorated by his explanation. Lit from the inside out.

"And I had the financial freedom to do it. I started my own gallery and traveled around the country looking for talented kids. I'd commission pieces, show them they could make money with their art, and then put entire shows together.

"It was quite a to-do at the beginning. The stuffy art types didn't like my unconventional methods; they thought artists and galleries should remain high-brow and all that rubbish. And commissioning pieces from kids . . .?" His voice lilted upwards as he raised his eyebrows.

Beth interjected, in her best New York accent, "Forget about it!"

His face split into a grin. "Forget about it!" he tried, and failed at the accent.

"Eventually, though, the art world accepted me and then, as they are wont to do, claimed that they thought it was a brilliant idea from the start. The heads of the most prestigious galleries praised my efforts. It was a gas."

"That's so . . . Zen of you. I would have gutted them." She shook her head at the hypocrisy, the injustice.

With a knowing look, he said, "I'm sure you would have."

"Now," he continued, "the organization has grown significantly. I have donors and fundraisers and five galleries throughout England promoting young artists."

"Wow." Beth was impressed. "That's amazing," she said, genuinely surprised by the life her dashing, but not exactly serious friend had created.

"I'm proud of you, Wes," she said with affection.

He sat back, looking like a boy who'd been given a gold star. "Ta," he said, letting her see how pleased he was by her words.

"And as it happens, I have my biggest event of the year on Saturday. I was going to wait until the close of the night, but . . . will you come?"

"With *you?*"

"Well, yes. That *is* the general idea."

"What? Did your date drop you at the last minute?" she teased nervously.

"No, I wasn't planning on taking anyone. I might have to pop off and make sure everything is running smoothly. I know you well enough to know that you'll be just fine on your own. Probably hold court with all of your admirers."

She scrunched her nose together. "*My admirers?*"

"Yes, you can be quite beguiling, Elizabeth." His eyes were now boring into hers, willing her to get some meaning, some truth. It made her even more nervous. "Well? Will you come?"

He probably meant it as a platonic date. A friendly invitation to accompany him. Still, her answer was almost a whisper. "Yes."

Wes sat back, looking extraordinarily pleased with himself, like he'd just won something.

He knew her well enough to change the subject quickly. He didn't want to give her the opportunity to overanalyze the situation and retract her acceptance. "Tell me, then, what was it like seeing Audre?" He took another bite of his food.

Beth shook her head, trying to switch gears. "It was yesterday. It was good and . . . exhausting?"

He nodded. "She laid into you, didn't she?"

Beth eyes flashed. "Of course she did, but I deserved it."

"She was pretty livid with you for cutting her out of your life," he confirmed.

There it was again. The truth she couldn't run away from.

Suddenly she was curious about what he thought. "Why aren't you angry with me?"

He shrugged. "It's life. But I also had an inkling that you would come around eventually."

"You did?"

"Oh, yes, I'm quite wise. Didn't you know?"

She pressed her lips together and stifled a smile.

"No, in all seriousness, I knew I'd see you again. You loved London too much to stay away. And the world being as small and as connected as it is, fate was bound to bring you back to me."

Her voice quivered. "Fate?"

He nodded. His words were heavy, but his tone was light. She held on to the light.

"As I was saying, catching up with Audre was exhausting, but not because she was angry with me." She searched for the right words. "It was exhausting because for the first time I could see what it must have been like for my friends. The people I cared about, who cared about me. How awful and callous I must have seemed to ignore the phone calls and emails."

She looked down, completely ashamed again. "I was only thinking of myself, consumed with each new case. There was nothing else. I just abandoned everything and everyone."

The emotion was overwhelming. She felt like a failure and a terrible person.

Worse. A disappointment.

In all her thirty-five years, she'd never felt like a disappointment. She was smart, dedicated, well-liked, and she excelled in all things.

Now realizing that she was disappointed in herself, she bit back the tears.

Looking up at Wes with shimmering eyes, she said, "I'm sorry." She said it to him, but she was really talking to herself.

"No." He shook his head. "No, don't apologize. You don't have anything to be sorry about."

He reached across the table to cradle her face in one hand; his thumb swept up the single tear that fell.

She leaned into his hand. Giving in to the warmth of it, the comfort.

He searched her face, reading it. "You aren't alone, Liz."

"Yes, I am. Mags is gone and I've pushed everyone away," she said in a small voice.

He narrowed his eyes. "No you haven't."

The pained look on his face transformed into something else. Resolve?

"Now up you get; it's time for a dance." Wes grabbed Beth's hand and pulled her up with him. "This situation requires immediate levity—or, as you were once very fond of saying, *enough of the heavy.*"

Chapter 7: First Kisses

They danced the Lindy and the Charleston, the Foxtrot and the Tango.

Wes was a great dancer, partly because growing up in certain circles in England meant he couldn't escape some formal training, and partly because Beth had dragged him to classes during their London summer.

They moved together easily to the measured tempo of "Puttin' on the Ritz," the high tempo of "Remarkable Girl," and the thumping bass and blaring trumpets of "The Sheik of Araby."

Finally winded, they grabbed a small round table just off the dance floor that hadn't existed five minutes before. Looking around, Beth noticed more tables popping up, with chairs on one side only facing the stage.

As they danced, she'd remembered more and more of their summer together. How much fun they'd had. How easily the friendship came.

Audre's words, too, had echoed in her brain as they danced. The more she considered it, the more she saw the truth of what she'd said.

Abruptly, she turned her eyes on him, ready to study his reaction. "Wes, did you like me?"

She had his attention.

His mouth went slack. "*Like* you?"

"Yes, were you romantically interested in me then?"

Without hesitation he answered, "Unequivocally."

There was nothing but truth in his eyes.

She needed to be direct. They'd reached that stage where it was pointless to act coy. "Then why didn't you kiss me?"

"Because . . . you were intimidating. You're still intimidating," he admitted. He was surprised by her candid approach, but gratified that she wasn't sidestepping their attraction any longer.

"*How?*" she pressed.

He considered his words carefully. "When you look at me, there's no pretense, no ulterior motive. You're just *you* . . . looking through me."

"And that's intimidating?"

"Yes. There aren't many people who can or will do that in the world. At least not in England."

She stopped. Considering whether she really wanted to know the answer to the next question. "And do you like me now?" she prodded, surprising herself with how self-possessed she sounded.

"What are we, in primary?" he chided, half of his face turning up in a sexy grin that made her mouth water.

She narrowed her eyes. "Just answer the ques—"

"Yes." He cut her off. "Yes, I like you." He let the full force of his eyes come down on her. Willing her to understand. To believe. To trust him.

He didn't ask her why she was suddenly being so forward. Beth wasn't entirely sure herself. She had a sneaking suspicion it was a direct result of her having judged so poorly with Connor.

She'd been so certain of him. And yet, she'd gotten it all wrong.

It was important to be on the same page with Wes.

The logic in her brain gave way to the intensity in Wes' gaze. The chairs were arranged so that they were sitting next to each other; he was leaning in.

She was ready . . . at least for this one indulgence. Deliberately, she gave in to the pull to be closer, to finally feel his lips.

Just as they were about to close the distance, a disembodied voice came over the speakers.

"Lords and Ladies, or should I say Flappers and Sheiks. . . ." Wes exhaled; it was a frustrated kind of sound. They both turned to the stage.

"Now presenting the beautiful, the dazzling, the talented . . . Miss Coco La Rouge."

All the guests were seated now at the newly erected tables set facing the stage.

A spotlight focused on the edge of the floor.

A muted trumpet blared from somewhere nearby. Light from a spotlight focused on a column just off the stage.

A single bejeweled leg appeared from behind it, slow and seductive.

And then a woman in a black knee-length pea coat approached the stage, one sultry step at a time.

Her red heels accentuated the line of her legs as she walked up to the stage and sat on the French settee, following the winding notes of the trumpet.

Her hair was pinned up in a 1930s style; big dark curls framed her pale face and set off her red lips.

Carefully she removed her lace gloves one finger at a time, never breaking eye contact with the audience.

The atmosphere in the hall turned thick, lustful.

Coco stood up to remove her coat, one button at a time. She turned her back to the audience and exposed one arm, then looked over her naked shoulder seductively.

Every movement was deliberate, calculated for maximum effect.

Her dance made every woman feel sexy and powerful, and every man hungry for a taste.

Beth leaned forward into the table, clasping her hands loosely in front of her as she watched, drawn in by this woman and her powers.

She was like a prima ballerina, a maestra in the art of movement, but instead of inspiring awe, each calculated act as she turned to let the coat drop to her feet and expose her red bra and corset was meant to inspire desire.

Next to her, Beth could feel Wes move. With his eyes fixed on the stage, he leaned into her, taking one of her hands.

Slowly, deliberately, he pressed his palm into her, flattening her hand on the white linen, fingers down. Then he pulled it to the edge of the table.

When the tips reached the edge, he laced his fingers through hers all at once. The sudden possession caused her chest to rise and fall.

Her insides clenched together.

He brought her hand to rest on his thigh under the table, where he flipped it palm-side up like he was throwing her back onto the bed.

The heat rose in her. Her pulse throbbed against his palm as he moved his fingers lightly over her fate line, up from her wrist and down the middle towards her ring finger.

Coco had just undone her garter and had now turned her back on the audience to unlace her corset.

Her hand curled in on his probing digits. He pressed his weight into her again, forcing her to stay open.

Four of his fingers now grazed her palm.

Desire pooled in Beth; she was all feeling, all sensation. For the briefest of moments, she wondered whether the people sitting at the tables nearest them could know what was happening under their table.

The dancer finished with the corset, pivoting in one quick movement to unhook the front, her arms closing in on her body and then yanking the garment open. A trumpet and a drum punctuated the thud as the corset hit the floor.

She could feel his measured restraint as his fingers kissed the sensitive skin, delving into the hills and valleys up to where her fingers met her palm. From the corner of her eye, she could see him turn his eyes from the performer, fixing them instead on her face.

Coco was now down to her ruby-encrusted bra. She again turned her back to the audience so she could unhook it and draw out the tease.

She did it and swung around to face her admirers, bouncing breasts exposed.

Wes reached the delta of her hand at the same time, lacing his fingers through hers once more. Forcefully, he possessed her palm, letting her feel the full strength in his hands.

It felt like he'd just done something *else* to her.

She tried to control her breathing. Her pale skin flushed from the seemingly innocent contact.

The spotlight was extinguished and Coco took a bow, making her way off the stage.

She ventured a glance in Wes' direction. His jaw was tight, the muscles in his face constricted with some unseen effort. His eyes had narrowed; he wore a look she'd seen from him before, although nowhere near this intensity.

He was looking at her like she was mouthwatering.

Her breasts heaved, pressing against the satin of the dress.

"Fancy seeing you here." A man stood over them, snapping them out of the trance they'd created, severing the electricity flowing between them.

Wes looked at the man, blinking rapidly as the lust was forced away. She could see him visibly bite back his frustration and replace the passion with a polite smile. He stood to shake the man's hand. "And what shall we call you tonight, old chap?"

The man was older, in his forties, but very good-looking. Bits of gray gathered at his temples.

He leaned in, answering in a low, but mischievous voice. "Call me Winston."

"The British Bulldog?"

Winston's back straightened proudly. "Indubitably."

Wes nodded knowingly, a glint of humor in his eyes.

"And you, my good man? What is your nom de guerre for our little soirée?"

Wes turned to Beth and back to Winston reluctantly. "Apparently, tonight . . . I'm Art." His voice was thick with sarcasm and dry humor.

"Art?" Winston repeated with a dubious look and more than a little confusion.

"Art," Wes repeated in the same tone.

"Well. *Art.* I do believe your manners have left you— who is this ravishing creature you've been keeping to yourself all evening?" He looked to Beth appreciatively.

She returned his smile, the color rising for an instant as the novelty of picking the name hit her again. "Natasha," she answered. "Pleasure." They shook hands.

"Well, Natasha, I do hope I'll have the pleasure of seeing you at Art's *humble* gathering on Saturday," he said in his best sarcastic British tone.

Wes placed an arm around her shoulders possessively. "Yes, she's agreed to accompany me." He smiled wide, the message clear.

Winston seemed thrown by this bit of information. "Is that so? How unexpected. In all these years, there's never been anyone on your arm on the red carpet."

His manner of speaking would have made someone question his sexuality in the U.S., but Beth knew he was just very British. And then there was the matter of his roaming eyes...

"Red carpet?" Beth wondered out loud more to herself than them, remembering that everything was done up just so in London. Of course, Wes' event would be no exception.

"Oh yes, my dear. It's the social event of the spring!" Winston seemed eager to keep talking to them, but the band began playing again just as the tables were cleared away.

The opening notes of "Let's Do It" filled the hall.

Wes moved his hand down her arm until their fingers were laced together. "Oh, will you look at that. It's the Cole Porter song I promised you. Darling, I do believe I owe you a dance," he said, moving away from the man.

"Cheers then!" he called to Winston over his shoulder.

Winston gave them a short wave.

"What was that about?" Beth asked as Wes spun her into him, holding her closer than when they'd danced before.

"Let's just say *Winston* tends to prattle on. He's also a bit of a cad. If you see him on Saturday and I'm not with you, try not to let him corner you. He'll probably ask you to dance and then try to touch you inappropriately."

She stopped moving with him.

"Oh, don't worry, nothing too scandalous. It's just that if he were to try anything, I know what your response would be." His smile was knowing and wise.

"I'd break his hand." "You'd break his hand." They said the words together, and then laughed.

He did know her well.

"Something I hope can be avoided, as it is quite an important night for me," Wes said pointedly, but with affection in his voice.

Beth nodded. "If I see him coming, I'll run the other way."

They started dancing again. Wes spun her in several consecutive underarm turns. The thousand candles around the hall flickered in and out of view in a blur of golden light.

By one in the morning they were installed in Wes' car. They'd spent the rest of the night dancing and laughing. Nothing had changed between them, and yet everything had changed.

She was suddenly very grateful for the direction of the wind.

"Do you remember that night we broke into Kensington Gardens?" She rested her head against the seat, falling into the memory.

"You mean our night in Never Never Land." It wasn't a question. "Of course."

"How did that all start?" she asked, eyes still on the ceiling of the car.

He laughed. "I believe the way most of our shenanigans began . . . with a little whiskey."

She angled her head in his direction. "I remember we were all in your apartment, but how did we actually arrive at the decision to do it?"

He nodded, ready to give her the play-by-play she couldn't call to mind. "You felt like a wander. You were always wanting to wander." The affection in his eyes was so honest that it made the butterflies dance.

He continued in a soft voice, "We walked by the Gardens and you instantly began bouncing up and down at the idea of breaking in to see the Peter Pan statue. Then, a few seconds later, you had the brilliant idea for the photo. We returned to my flat to pick up a few torches and your camera, and then we were on our way."

"That's right." She remembered the missing pieces now. Since her reunion with Audre, she'd been trying to recall the whole memory.

She hadn't actually drank much that night, but for some reason the memory felt distant. Like it was on the other side of frosty glass.

She felt Wes still beside her. "And then after we'd cleared the guard, I cornered you against the ivy gate while Audre, Loryn, and Mark kept running." His voice was as smooth as velvet.

"We almost kissed that night," he finished, now looking at her lips.

Beth remembered. "But then we heard the guard still coming for us and we made our escape," she whispered.

The car stopped. They'd arrived back at No. 3.

Wes quickly got out, stopping first to whisper something to his driver, then around to open her door.

He took her hand, gallantly helping her out. Then the car drove off.

"He's just going around the block so we can have a proper goodnight," Wes explained before she could ask.

They waited for another car to pass before they started across the street.

Walking hand in hand up the steps to the landing, Beth felt like a teenager on a first date.

They walked up the steps and stopped in front of the door. Using the hand that held hers, he steered her until she was facing him. His free hand came to her face, lifting her chin up.

Her breathing became shallow as he asked permission with his eyes.

She could do this. She would allow herself this. She'd thought of him in this way over the years here and there—imagined what it would have been like. She was ready.

With the most imperceptible of nods, she consented.

The old street lamps reflected in his eyes, she could see the attachment there.

Slowly the world melted away. The sound of cars passing, of the city turning, doors opening and closing, the breeze rustling through the trees—it all ceased to matter as his lips finally met hers after fifteen years.

They were strong and pliable, at once molding to hers and demanding more. His arms wrapped around her back, until nothing but their clothes stood between them.

He deepened the kiss with the authority of a skilled lover, making her knees go weak. He enclosed her more tightly in the protection of his arms.

It was better than she had imagined.

She wrapped her arms around his neck, needing him to be closer. An involuntary sound of pleasure escaped her lips as he kissed her more urgently.

"Feckin' A!"

Beth's eyes shot open. Instinctively she pushed Wes away, letting her arms fall to her side.

Instantly recognizing the speaker, she slowly turned to find Connor Bannon standing in front of No. 3 Pembroke Rose.

Chapter 8: Past & Present

"What the f—" she started under her breath.

Her jaw had dropped, all semblance of composure gone.

The Irishman took a few stunned steps up the path, his face full of accusation.

Wes stepped in front of Elizabeth. "*Bannon*?!" he said with equal astonishment and contempt.

Connor stopped, narrowing his eyes. "Cartwright?" he answered, matching his tone.

Beth stepped out from behind Wes. "You two know each other?" She fought every impulse to scream.

"Cambridge," they said in unison, not looking at her.

"Are you fucking kidding me? There's like more than ten thousand undergraduates alone . . . and you guys aren't even the same year!" She wasn't sure why she was angry. Or rather, she wasn't sure what was making her *more* angry.

Was she angry because her first kiss with Wes had been interrupted? Because she felt guilty about it when she'd heard Connor's voice? Because it was awkward to be standing there with the two of them? Because she still felt the urge to kick Connor in the balls?

Maybe she was just angry at the Universe for converging in on her in that exact moment.

Connor and Wes stood staring at each other.

"The person you were seeing in Ireland was Bannon?" Wes turned to her, no judgment in his voice, only surprise.

She nodded, still radiating anger.

"What's he doing here?" His eyes never left her face.

She turned to Connor. "I have no idea," she said accusingly.

"Jaysus, woman, I leave the continent for two seconds and you cozy up with the likes of *him*?" His voice was full of derision. A hint of something briefly registered on his face and then it was gone. "That took no time at'all."

Elizabeth's eyes went wild.

Quickly, she reined it in. She wouldn't give him the satisfaction of showing how angry he'd made her.

That would imply that she cared he'd been off screwing a supermodel. Even as she thought it, she cringed.

She mustered the most convincing smile she was capable of. A mask. The one she used in the courtroom.

Turning to Wes, she was careful to sound genuine and true. "Art, I had a lovely time. *Thank you.*"

Flagrantly ignoring Connor, he took her hand. "Anytime, *Natasha*." He leaned in to kiss her on the cheek, letting his lips linger on her skin.

He broke away, resting his forehead against hers. "I'll pick you up at seven on Saturday."

The blood burned her skin. Whether it was because of the way his voice curled around every word or because Connor was standing there watching it all, she didn't know.

Wes released her and sauntered down the steps past Connor, not giving him a second glance. A few moments later, his car collected him and he was gone.

Beth turned to unlock the door.

"Seriously? No hallo for me?" He was angry. "And here you are snogging *Wes Cartwright*, after what? Only two weeks in England?"

He whistled low in his throat. "You sure do move fast, Lass."

She winced. He'd never called her lass. Only "luv" from the start. And it had been a while since he'd used anything but Lara.

She shook her head, choosing to let the sting fall away from her. *He had no right.*

With a cool calm she didn't feel, she turned on him. "Why hello, Mr. Bannon." Her Stepford wife delivery made him snap back.

"Isn't it a small world?" she continued. "Your knowing my good friend Wes, whom I've known for *fifteen* years!" She scrunched her nose at the fifteen for emphasis. "Isn't that just . . . wonderful?"

It bothered her more than she wanted to admit—that he could think she would move on with someone after only knowing them for two weeks. Like she'd just be able switch gears. Like he meant nothing to her. The same way she meant nothing to him. . . .

She turned the key in the lock and pushed the door open. "Well, it's been lovely seeing you again. Take care," she called over her shoulder.

"Elizabeth!" he scolded. "That's it? That's all I get?"

She turned to face him head-on. "Oh, I'm sorry, where are my manners?" Sticking with the Stepford tone seemed like the best idea.

Play the character, Beth. Don't let him see you sweat.

"When did you get back from your trip?"

"Last week." He was eyeing her suspiciously.

Like the tabloid claimed.

"Did you have a nice time?"

"Yes." He was searching her face for something.

She had no idea what it could possibly be.

"You've been keeping busy, I expect?" he asked in a flat tone, still trying to come to some conclusion.

"Oh, yes. Taking pictures, catching up with friends. . . ."

His face blanched.

"Catching up on the gossip rags. . . ." she said pointedly, letting the words hang in the air. She was pleased, at least, that she truly sounded unaffected. "They're really quite enlightening in this country."

For a moment it seemed his lips twitched up a degree, but then it was gone.

"Don't believe everything you read," he threw back.

"That's true." She nodded in agreement. "So wise. So wise. But you know what? Sometimes the truth is right there in front of your face." She shook her head lightly like it was the darnedest thing.

"Oh well." She shrugged. "I'm really quite tired. Good night, Mr. Bannon."

Connor's mask fell away in that moment. His eyebrows drew together. A flash of pain transformed his features. "*Lara?*"

She stepped inside and closed the door.

He knocked as she fell back against it, willing herself to let it go.

"Lara?" he said through the door. "Can't we talk about it, please?"

"There's nothing left to say," she answered simply.

"Lara!" He was more forceful.

"It's fine, Connor. We had no understanding. And a picture says a thousand words." She waited for him to say something, anything to refute her words, to explain.

Nothing.

Suddenly exhausted, she turned towards the door one last time. "Good night, Mr. Bannon."

She walked through the foyer and up the stairs without waiting for an answer. Reminding herself that the wind had carried her in a different direction . . . towards someone else.

CHAPTER 9: ROWLING IN AUSTEN

The following day, Beth woke early and made her morning smoothie to the news, blasting the blender through most of the stories.

There was never any good news.

A ninety-year-old grandmother of three robbed at gunpoint. A woman with spiky dark hair seen on CCTV breaking into a room at the Ritz. A man takes his life after losing his job.

She sent all the people mentioned positive thoughts and then turned off the TV. It was too depressing. She'd have to consider cutting the news out of her life completely.

The blacks and grays had colored too much of her world already. Enough to last a lifetime. No more.

She poured the green contents into her "jolly good" pint glass and cleaned the blender out before sitting down in front of her laptop at the table on the terrace.

After reading a few uplifting stories on goodnewsnetwork.org, she turned her attention to the day.

Shopping for Saturday's gala was at the very top of her list and so she readied herself for the legwork required to find what she was looking for.

It was a relief to escape into such things. To not think about last night. To go through the superficial motions of finding a beautiful dress to wear.

She lost herself in the colors and fabrics of Gucci, Chanel, and Louis Vuitton—all of which were located just around the corner from No. 3.

She picked up a few things, but nothing that quite fit the occasion. The dress had to be formal, modestly sexy, and she wanted it to be youthful and artistic as well.

It was a very specific look which she finally found in a boutique carrying Reem Acra. Beth had told the sleek-looking manager what she needed and why she needed it. The well-coiffed woman's eyes had gone wide at the mention of Wes' event. "I'm going to my friend's art fundraiser tomorrow night," she had said. The manager, whose cool blonde hair was pinned back in an updo, asked for the name of the organization and when Beth mentioned it absently while fingering a lovely ivory gown on display in the boutique, the woman took her by the elbow and ushered her into the back room where she presented her with the perfect garment.

The dress had a gold lace, high-collar bodice that ended in an A-line seam, partially covering a long medium sky blue satin chiffon gown with a sweetheart neckline.

A decadent splurge. It was quite possibly the most stunning thing she'd ever owned. Dreamy, more feminine than any of her other formal gowns—she couldn't wait to wear it.

She'd stopped in at a few upscale local shops as well, buying a tall pillar candle that smelled of lemon and sage. She also found a beautiful wind chime made from an array of colorful crystals.

The store, London Glass, caught her eye as she made her way back to No. 3. She'd spent her time happily examining the gleaming glassware in the window, her arms full of the day's purchases. She'd almost resolved to buy a set with a unique Celtic knot pattern etched in the bottom of the glass, when she caught sight of a man with a camera across the street. Initially she'd thought he was a tourist, but his lens had been pointed at the store for longer than would have been natural for a sightseer.

She picked up a glass, balancing all of her purchases in the other hand. She pretended to examine the bottom, but she was really studying the man dressed in elegant black pants and a beautifully cut indigo shirt. Definitely not a tourist. Paparazzi. . . ? He was dressed too well.

She shook her head, setting the glass down as the man started walking back up the street. She was getting paranoid. Her imagination had started to get away from her. At times it felt like London had eyes. She scolded herself and went immediately back to No. 3.

After putting her new purchases safely away, she got down to the business of finding someone to come and do her hair and makeup. She was genuinely surprised that she'd never thought to hire someone to do that for her in California.

It was nice not having to think about the colors and the pins and the hair spray.

She booked her appointment for five the following day and went to her room to change into a pair of comfortable yoga pants.

Staying in for a quiet night seemed like a good way to end the week of reconnections and drama.

Upon returning, she felt the chill in the air coming through the open terrace doors. She crossed the room and closed them.

Turning back towards the library nook, she considered the massive collection.

Apparently, Sarah didn't believe in organizing her books in any discernible way. She had J.R. Ward's *Dark Lover* next to *Men Are from Mars and Women Are from Venus.* Her fingers traced the cover of *Siddhartha,* which sat next to *Twilight.*

Her eyes fell to the shelf just below eye level.

Jane Austen. Maybe it was a Jane Austen kind of night.

. . .

She examined the book next to it, *Harry Potter and the Philosopher's Stone.* A seemingly odd choice next to *Pride and Prejudice,* and yet in this one instance, Beth understood her host well.

Her phone started buzzing from somewhere near the couches. She looked to the coffee table where she expected it to be. Nothing.

As she neared the sound she realized that it was muted, quieter. Like it wasn't vibrating against a hard surface.

She knelt to stick her hands in between the cushions of the couch until at last she fished it out. But she was too late; the phone had stopped, and then buzzed once more.

A voice mail.

She swiped the screen and registered the number. Her knees gave a little. She let the couch catch her.

Connor.

Why couldn't he just leave her alone? It was over. Run its course. Their story had been destined to be brief. And she was fine with it.

Or at least working towards fine.

And then there was the wind. . . .

Her hand pulsed with dread and, if she was being honest, *excitement*, as she put the phone to her ear to listen to the message.

"Lara." It was a caress.

She swallowed.

"I'm sorry for the way I behaved last night. It wasn't my intention . . . I just . . . well, it was a bit of a shock.

"I need to see you.

"Please.

"Call me."

Her face burned. Hearing his voice in her ear . . . it took her back to when his lips had been very at home there.

When his words could make her unravel in delicious waves.

Back when she was still living in Fantasyland.

She placed the phone down beside her and sunk into the couch, letting her head fall back.

She hugged herself. How had she gotten it so wrong? She'd given him the opportunity to explain when she'd mentioned the picture—if indeed there was an explanation. Her heart sank as she remembered his guilty silence.

The phone buzzed.

A text.

Reluctantly, she looked.

I need to see you.

She felt nauseated; her breathing was too shallow.

And then the phone buzzed again in her hand. Another text popped up.

Please. -Connor

Ugh! What right did he have? Why did he even want to see her? Wasn't he content with his supermodel?

He was probably bored with her already.

On to the next. . . .

"NO!" She raised her voice, directing it at a painting hanging between the two windows that faced the street. A replica of Chagall's *I and the Village* depicting a white horse staring at a green-faced man.

She was determined not to give in to her emotions. Not the irrational pull to answer his text, or the indignant anger that made her want to hit something.

The phone buzzed again.

"Oh, for *fuck's* sake!"

She threw the phone into the cushions, now seething.

After a minute of sneaking glances in its direction, like someone would see her—judge her for even considering it—she finally gave in and swiped the screen.

Mercifully, it was a text from Audre.

Hey Babes! You, me, Loryn tonight. Have plans already? Don't care . . . I am brilliant and need to be toasted to—girls night/reunion is in order . . . plus there's, you know, the simple matter of your having to MAKE UP FOR A DECADE. Coach & Horses in Soho at 7.

Suddenly, a quiet night in with her thoughts and a potentially vibrating phone seemed like the last thing she needed.

A night with the girls? Yes, please.

Can I wear jeans? Beth texted her friend.

Audre responded instantly.

You may feel out of place, but then again, you can just chalk it up to being American.

She'd take that chance. A night with the girls in casual wear? Perfect.

In.

Audre's text came in one second after she hit send.

Brill. Ask to be let upstairs at the bar.

CHAPTER 10: SECRET TEA & GREAT WHITES

An hour later she was outside the red exterior of the Coach & Horses. Without stopping to admire the decor she walked inside and approached the barman. She was about to ask to be let upstairs when he looked up from the paper in his hand and took in her ivory blouse top, skinny jeans, and boots.

Without a word, he motioned up the stairs behind the bar with a knowing smile.

Audre had told him she was coming. "She'll look like an American," she must have warned him.

Once on the narrow stairs, Beth felt like she'd stepped back in time. The wooden boards creaked under her feet, and the railing was worn and smooth. But it was more than that; it was quiet up here with the muted sounds of old music flowing down from above.

Once on the landing she understood. The sign said "Soho's Secret Tea Room."

She was greeted by a woman in a red dress with a white collar and a 1940s hairstyle.

Loryn and Audre were seated at a table by the window.

The small tables, homey fireplace, and original wood floors made it feel like stepping back into your grandmother's living room—if your grandmother was a well-to-do Londoner that lived several decades ago.

There was no one else there.

"Darling!" Audre stood to kiss her on both cheeks. She wore a sleek black dress that looked just as out of place in the quaint surroundings as Beth's skinny jeans.

Loryn stood up, smiling from ear to ear. "Liz!"

Elizabeth hugged her old friend. She was taller than Beth, but shorter than Audre. Her blonde hair was pulled back in an elegant ponytail, and her dress was a form-fitting pale blue.

Finally, they sat down. "So what is this place?"

"Didn't you see the sign?"

"Soho's Secret Tea Room?"

Audre gave her a wry smile. "Oh, well spotted," she teased.

"I mean why are we the only ones here?" Beth prodded. "And why does it feel like we're on a movie set for a period drama?"

"Well, that's their thing, Luv. A vintage-inspired tea room. But it closes at six. I hired them for dinner; that's why there's no one else here. I thought we three deserved a proper catch-up," Audre finished.

"So we aren't having tea?" Beth sounded disappointed.

"You can still have it, just with a spot of dinner as well."

Beth searched the small table for the menus. Loryn's shoulders rose with a laugh, giving her a *did you forget who we're with* look.

Right.

Audre was beaming back at her.

"You've already ordered for us, haven't you." It wasn't a question.

The lady in the red dress was back with a separate pot of tea for everyone and slices of cake.

Beth gave Audre a questioning look. She just shrugged. "Knowing your penchant for sweets, I thought we would start with dessert tonight."

The server arranged everything around them.

Audre explained, "Your pot is a rooibos. I know you usually take Earl Grey, but this will go best with the cheese and berry sponge cake. Which, to be quite honest, will be your favorite treat in London and the entire reason I chose this place."

"You chose this place because you knew I'd love the cake?" Elizabeth almost teared up. Some people would always know you. . . .

Audre nodded, completely sure of herself. "You're welcome."

Beth turned her attention to Loryn. "OK, Lo, fill me in. Dree said you're a buyer for Topshop?"

Loryn shook her head. "Eh, no, nice try. You're the one who went away. You first." She crossed her arms and pursed her lips.

Her best attempt at looking miffed.

Loryn wasn't the angry type. Of the three of them, she was the gentle one. The one to forgive and forget. But she held her drawn eyebrows in place. Her pursed lips didn't budge either.

Beth held up her hands and sat back. "I'm sorry, OK? I suck. I completely suck as a friend *and* as a human being. . . ." And so she launched into her spiel for the third time.

This time she was able to repeat it with virtually no emotional minefields. Got through it unscathed. *Almost.*

Loryn then filled in the gaps to her story. About becoming a buyer, what her days looked like. She told Beth about getting married to a nice man named James and how she'd built herself a lovely little life.

She was just as she remembered her: sweet, upbeat, and kind.

"Congratulations, Lo! You must be really happy." Beth reached across the table to squeeze Loryn's hand.

"Yes, thanks. I am." There was a hard edge to her words. "I am . . . really very happy." It sounded like she was trying to convince herself of that fact.

"Lo?"

Her smile had turned a little crazed, a little Stepford.

She just shook her head. "No, yeah. I am—I am really happy."

Audre's face had scrunched together. "You already said that, Babes."

They both studied her now.

Loryn tried to hold on to her smile. It wavered.

"Are you OK?" Beth asked, suddenly concerned.

Loryn's face cracked, her body collapsed forward, and she put her elbows on the table.

Just as Beth was about to be seriously alarmed, going through a checklist of what would be done if he was abusive or if she needed help getting out, Lo looked up at them.

"It's just that . . . sometimes he drives me *completely barmy!*" Her voice rose with the last word. Losing her composure, she let it all hang out. "Like how he just leaves his dirty garments *everywhere.* I mean, honestly? Honestly? What's that about? And then there's the whole bit where I'll never be alone again. . . ."

Loryn launched herself into a tirade of typical marriage complaints that seemed to have been weighing on her. Nothing at all serious, just signs that they were going through an extended adjustment period one year in.

And Loryn was much too polite and passive-aggressive to explain it to her husband.

After she was through, Lo took a deep cleansing breath. "Oh, God, what a bloody relief. I've just been walking around telling everyone how blissfully happy I've been. It's so exhausting."

Loryn looked equal parts relieved and embarrassed that she'd allowed herself to crack. Beth wanted to let her off the hook, change everyone's focus, but she wasn't sure if she had anything to offer.

Suddenly Audre grinned. "So, ladies, there was actually a *second* reason I asked you out. You see...." She took a dramatic pause. More than a pause; she just stopped, letting her audience wait.

Beth leaned forward, excited to hear her friend's news. Sufficiently certain that she had their attention, Dree continued, "I am completely and totally brilliant. Honestly, I am. It is a truth universally known."

"What is it? Out with it, Dree." Beth almost kicked her under the table. She was taking her bloody dramatic time, even for Audre.

"My *brilliance* is only matched by my friends," she continued cryptically.

They waited.

"Elizabeth, darling, do you remember that meeting for my exhibition?"

Beth nodded.

"Well, for a variety of reasons I won't go into now, we had a massive cock-up and lost *three* pieces, which is essentially an entire wall of the exhibit. And the judging happens this Wednesday with a semi-formal gala a week from tomorrow."

"*OK?*" Beth said slowly, shaking her head, willing her friend to get to the point.

"I am brilliant, you see, because I fixed said problem . . . *magically.*" Her eyes danced with mischief.

Even Loryn was losing patience. "What are you prattling on about? Just get on with it."

"The show is the Natural History Museum's annual Wildlife Photographer of the Year exhibit. It's one of our biggest draws, really prestigious. Going on fifty years now."

Beth knew the direction they were headed in. *For her wall*, she remembered.

"The gist is that I presented your photograph of Fungie and the great white and the committee went completely barmy for it. They loved it, Beth."

Elizabeth bit her lip, trying to take the compliment without splitting into a goofy grin. She could guess where this was going.

"So, even though submissions closed and the finalists were chosen *months* ago, the rules do give the committee and the curator," she pointed to herself, "leeway to put the show together and make adjustments where needed."

Beth opened her mouth to point out the obvious ethical problems with Audre's solution, but as usual, Audre read her face.

She held up her hands. "I was completely upfront with the committee. I explained our friendship and that you'd given me permission to use it in whatever capacity I saw fit, but that you didn't know I was submitting it for their consideration. They didn't have a problem with it."

Beth took a deep breath. Something rose up in her stomach. It was somewhere between butterflies and chills. Like she'd just stumbled on a blue butterfly of her very own.

"So, Babes, you are . . . *officially* . . . a finalist for Wildlife Photographer of the Year!"

Beth didn't have time to say anything because the server appeared as if on cue, glasses of champagne in hand. They each grabbed one.

"Cheers!" They clanged together.

"Wow," Beth breathed. "That's . . . I don't even— that's *amazing*, Dree. Thanks for thinking of me."

"Thinking of you?! I almost wet my knickers when I saw that photo. You're saving me, Babes. In a *huge* way. So I gather you don't have any objections to your newfound photography career, now officially being launched on Wednesday?"

Beth shook her head slowly from side to side and exchanged a radiant smile with both of her friends.

Just then her phone buzzed in the back pocket of her jeans.

She ignored it.

Audre began explaining what would happen next. How she'd need to come to the museum on Monday and inspect what they had done. Write something about the photo for their literature and then prepare a two-minute presentation on how she came to capture the photograph. The presentation would be for the final judging round on Wednesday night.

Her phone vibrated again.

Beth kept listening to Audre as she launched into how amazing it would be for Beth. She tried to focus on what she was saying, but then her phone buzzed *again*.

Her thoughts went to Connor.

Audre stopped mid-sentence. "Do you need to get that, Luv?"

Beth waved it off. "No, no, sorry. Continue."

But then her phone buzzed a fourth time.

Beth's shoulders fell. Giving in, she extracted the phone, fully intending to put it on complete silence.

Several texts.

Oh, great.

Elizabeth, I got your number from Kilian who got it from Mona.

It's Bree.

Beth didn't have time to wonder how Mona had gotten her number.

Bree hit send after each line, so each was a separate text.

I just wanted to tell you about something that happened today.

For a moment, all the blood drained from Beth's body. Instantly, she thought something had happened to Connor.

Her heart was in her throat.

But then she read on.

That scoundrel who held you at gunpoint?

Stephen?

131

He was released today from the hospital having completed his treatment.

No one here wanted to alarm you, but I thought you should know.

You know, just in case. Just have your wits about you. They say he's recovered, but you just never know.

Take care. -Bree

Beth must have looked alarmed, because her friends turned to her. Audre reached over to put a hand on her arm.

She let out a breath. After thinking something had happened to Connor, the news about Stephen wasn't all that alarming. She recovered herself easily.

"It's nothing." Beth shrugged, deeply relieved. She wasn't concerned he'd been released, although some part of her brain wondered if her blasé attitude on the subject was wise.

It would be fine. But it was clear from her friends' faces that she wouldn't be able to move on until they knew.

She told them about the greasy-haired twenty-something, Stephen, who'd grabbed her at a dance in Dingle. How she'd publicly humiliated him when she'd defended herself and how he'd come after her with a gun.

When she got to the part where she threw the knife to sever his tendons, they both jumped back in their seats like she was a storyteller and she'd just gotten to the climax.

She explained how Connor had wanted to nail his ass to the floorboards, and how Beth had intervened, making sure that he was sent to a mental health facility instead of a prison.

When she'd finally finished, she sat back and let out a deep breath.

Audre and Loryn were gobsmacked.

It was Audre who spoke first. "Chrrrist, Liz. You dated *Connor Bannon*, were held at *gunpoint*, and nearly eaten by a *great white—all* in the same month!"

Well, not exactly in the same month. But she didn't correct her friend.

Audre let out a low whistle. "That's it! We're going to get smashed after dinner and then dance our arses off at silent disco. It's decided." Her head bopped up and down dramatically, champagne glass in hand.

"Silent disco?"

Audre waved a dismissive hand and downed the rest of her champagne. "You'll love it."

She looked to Loryn, who was nodding eagerly.

Beth remembered Wes' event, "Speaking of dancing, do you guys have any etiquette tips for me? I'm going to Wes' big fundraiser thing tomorrow night." She took a sip of her champagne.

Audre looked beside herself. She smacked her hands down on the table, making the china rattle. "Oh. My. God. He's *taking* you? He never takes *anyone*. It's the most exclusive ticket in town! Ten thousand a plate!"

Beth was a little frightened by the force of Audre's reaction. She was *really* excited for her.

"Oh my God! Oh my God!" She almost hyperventilated.

Beth gave her a *what the hell is wrong with you* look.

Which only made Audre more impatient to convey her excitement. "You don't get it, Babes! When I say exclusive and hottest ticket, I mean even Her Majesty, the Queen, will be attending. And the fact that Wes is taking you as his *date*?!" Her voice finished an octave higher from where it had started.

Audre let out a girlish squeal.

Now Beth was terrified.

She wasn't sure which part scared her more: how convinced Audre was that Wes' invitation meant something significantly more than just a date—she was making it seem like a declaration of love—or the fact that the Queen herself would be in attendance. Was her Reem Acra gown elegant enough?

Suddenly, she felt an urge to go back to No. 3 and study. What, exactly, she wasn't sure.

Beth looked down at her cake, noticing it for the first time. She was ravenous after all of that storytelling.

She took a bite.

The tart and sweet flavors hit her tongue. The moist cake worked beautifully with the tang of the fruit and cheese frosting. She brought her free hand down on the table, rattling the china like Audre had done. Her head fell back and her eyes rolled as she let out a very loud foodgasm sound.

Much to Audre's delight.

Her friends laughed as Beth proceeded to inhale the rest of her cake.

Chapter 11: Missing Ireland

She woke the next morning feeling sore from her night of exuberant dancing with the girls. Silent disco had turned out to be outrageously fun.

They'd gone up to the top floor of a high rise. All four sides of the building were made of glass and provided the most spectacular views of London. Tower Bridge, the Eye, Big Ben. . . .

The experience of arriving was the strangest part. The room was filled to the brim with posh young people in their early twenties to their early fifties. They were all dressed in their own unique way. There were stylish updos and pink hair and dreads. Designer dresses and vintage and avant-garde styles that belonged on the runway. They all pulsed together to the music, but the room was dead silent.

The women were given headphones. They put them on and began vibrating at the same frequency as the rest of the room. The upbeat music blasted directly into their ears.

Colored lights flashed into the crowd. Some people wore luminescent jewelry and glowing lights in their hair.

It felt like another planet. The three friends left it all on the dance floor, leaving their stress and the drama and the cares of the world behind.

Elizabeth smiled up at the ceiling above her bed as she remembered. It had been better than sex—with John, anyway. Not. . . .

She stopped herself. But she *couldn't* stop herself completely. She settled for guiding her thoughts. She went from thinking of Connor, to thinking of her time in Ireland, to thinking of the other friends she'd made.

Mona. Kilian. Bree. Kait.

It was a relief to learn that she could steer her thoughts. Guide them to a safe place.

She thought of the little round woman with fading red hair and kind personality. It had been almost three weeks since they'd spoken. Mona had been delighted Elizabeth had made the effort to go back for her final night in Ireland to attend her sixtieth birthday party.

It had been a lovely evening filled with music and dancing and friends and conversation. She'd been grateful to have Kilian as a dance partner for most of the night.

They'd talked about his music and his songwriting. He'd had a productive month. Elizabeth, Kait, and Shaun had all stuck around the harbour listening to his songs late into the night.

Kil had been pleased to find a constructive critic in Beth. She pointed out places where the chorus could go in a different direction, making it stronger, or offered suggestions for the lyrics. They were an excellent creative team. He'd been emboldened by her helpful critique and crossed over into that flow state artists sometimes fell into, where the light touches their eyes and they tap in to something outside of themselves—reach a higher plane.

Elizabeth suddenly felt homesick. She missed her Irish friends. Missed the harbour lights reflecting on the Atlantic.

She extended an arm out on her bed, blindly searching for her cell. Her fingers found the smooth glass. She hit the side button to check the time; the thin white numbers revealed that it was past noon. She'd slept the morning away.

She sat up, leaning against the soft headboard as she dialed Mona's number.

"Hallo, Elizabeth!" she answered on the third ring.

For an instant Beth was surprised she knew it was her calling. She'd forgotten that Bree had told her that Mona already had her number—how that was true she still didn't know, but it didn't matter.

A healthy dose of color flushed Elizabeth's cheeks as she heard the tiny woman's pleasant voice.

"Hiya Mona," she said, smiling into the phone.

"How are things?" Mona asked, raising her voice over some clamor. It sounded like she was having lunch at the pub.

"Good, how are you? Have you made it out to the dance show in Galway yet?" Beth asked, referring to the eclectic show she'd seen on her tour of Ireland. It featured ballet, acrobatics, silks, and traditional Irish dancing. She'd purchased two tickets and a voucher for a stay at a local hotel as Mona's birthday present. The tickets weren't for a specific date, but the show was scheduled to close by mid-June.

"No, not yet! Cailin and I are planning to go in a fortnight, though. I'm very excited!" Elizabeth could hear Mona bounce on the other end. "It was so very kind a gift. Thank you again!"

Beth assured her that it was no great thing and then the two fell easily into conversation.

Mona told her about how Barry the Baker and Susan the Postmistress had had a huge row in front of everyone outside of Mollie's Chocolates. She launched into another story about some townsfolk Beth had never met, catching only parts of the story because the pub was so noisy.

After she was through with all the gossip, Mona informed her that Kilian had just stopped by her table to ask about Beth.

"Here, here, lad! Ask her yourself," she heard Mona say before Kilian's deep voice came on the line. "Liz!"

The noise of the pub seemed to fade, like he was walking outside.

"Hey, Kil!" She was happy to hear his voice. And yet it made something inside her chest ache. "How are things?" she asked him.

"Feckin' fantastic, they are. I've written three new songs—I can't wait for you to hear 'em. Especially this one that I think could be great—my best yet—but there's somethin' missing from the opening and the chorus isn't what

I'd like it to be. . . ." He recounted his last few weeks and how he felt like something was waking up inside him.

She'd never heard him so excited. Like he was finally realizing his potential.

"Jaysus, listen to me go on. How are ya, Liz? How's London?"

Beth responded in kind, telling him about reconnecting with her friends and silent disco and her burgeoning photography career. He was especially excited to hear about the photo of Fungie.

"That was a bleedin' barmy day, wasn't it?" He remembered looking over her shoulder at the photograph and then at the enormous creature as it approached the boat and then swam away again. "I thought it was going to charge at us! I kept thinkin' how I was going to explain to Connor that you'd been eaten by a shark—assuming I survived, of course. I'm sure he would have bitten my head off!"

Beth went silent as soon as he'd mentioned Connor.

"He doesn't know, does he?" Kilian was suddenly weary.

"No. . . ," she answered quickly.

"How is our lad?" he asked, changing the subject.

"I don't know," she answered with the least amount of emotion possible for her, keeping her voice steady.

"Haven't you seen him?" He was confused.

"Briefly." Beth didn't want to think about the exchange again.

He was silent. She could hear him thinking, trying to read between the lines. Or at least that's what she imagined he was doing as the seconds ticked by.

Her voice was measured. "I've got to go, Kil, OK?" she said, breaking the silence.

"Sure." He sounded concerned. "Hey, could you have a listen to that song I was telling you about? I can email it to you."

"Yeah, that sounds good." She gave him her email. "I have something today so I might not get around to it until Sunday."

"Yeah, no, that's fine. Take a week or two. I'm busy working on a new set anyway—don't stress about it."

They said their goodbyes. Kilian promised to give Mona a hug for her.

Elizabeth pressed the "end" button and sank back into the bed. Kilian's voice, his mentioning Connor, the silent concern on the other end of the line. . . . It had sent her down a spiral that made her feel ill.

She focused on steering her thoughts again, choosing to focus on Bree. She navigated to the texts her friend had sent the night before. Elizabeth quickly thanked her for the heads-up about Stephen and apologized for not responding immediately. She hit "send" and sank another degree.

Her thoughts gravitated towards Connor again and so she forced them in the direction of something she knew would hold her attention. She thought of Stephen. She wondered if he'd be able to stay clean after leaving treatment, wondered if he really was better, how he'd gotten to that desperate point in the cottage, and what lay ahead for him.

She was suddenly very curious about his story. She thought about him one-dimensionally, like a photograph. She wondered what needed to be done in his life to draw out his image—his true image. She hoped he had someone to help him. She hoped he had somewhere to go besides his father's.

Her eyes found the laptop on the nightstand to her right. She opened it and did something she never did . . . she searched for Stephen on Facebook. She vaguely recognized the first search suggestion that popped up and clicked on him.

His profile picture looked like it had been taken several years ago. He was virtually unrecognizable. His cheeks were filled in; his eyes didn't have that sunken, sallow quality to them; his smile was bright. He looked almost handsome. He was nineteen or twenty.

There were two other people in his profile picture, one on either side of him. An older man with gray hair and a fit physique, and a young man who looked the same age as Stephen. They had similar smiles and the same color hair. Behind them was a small mountain range, and something that looked like a vineyard.

There was nothing else to see; his settings were turned up to the highest privacy level. Only his profile picture was public.

Her phone buzzed on the bed next to her. It was Bree.

No problem, Liz.

I hope you're having a craic in London.

Met any dashing chaps you can pass on to me?

She considered that. She knew her friend was bi, of course, but she thought she preferred women.

Nope, sorry, Bree. They're Brits anyway, probably a bit stuffy for your taste, she teased.

Oh, I don't know about that. I bet I could crack them wide open with my charms.

I bet you could! Beth answered.

Bree excused herself, ending their brief text chat.

Elizabeth's eyes returned to the Facebook screen in front of her. A nervous feeling settled in her stomach. It rose up, making her mouth go dry. She swallowed.

She was suddenly itching to search for someone else. She sat there, a silent war raging in her head. Some judgmental part of her brain was disgusted she'd even had the thought, and disappointed that the urge to type in his name was growing stronger and stronger by the second.

She flexed her fingers, willing them not to settle on the keyboard. Her chest began to rise and fall too quickly; the blood rushed into her ears as she resisted.

Her fingers balled into fists, and her knuckles went bone-white as she held her breath. The urge had taken on a life of its own. Her brain was sending signals to her fingers: *do it, do it.* . . . Her conscious mind was screaming, *NO! NO! NO!*

Elizabeth didn't know how many minutes passed as she lay in bed, her laptop on her stomach, her fingers suspended in midair.

Finally, she gave in. She typed in his name and clicked on his picture.

His sapphire eyes assaulted her. Elizabeth recognized the mountain range in the background; he was somewhere in Tibet. Her heart thumped loudly throughout her body, pumping blood into every nook and cranny.

His job title read: *Adventurer, Wanderer, Collector.* She scrolled down. There were only a handful of public pictures. One of Kilian and him at Dingle Harbour. One of a tall grass field filled with animals somewhere in Africa. One of a slightly younger Connor standing outside of his college in Cambridge.

The final picture was clearly taken when he was in college. It was a group photo of Bram, Bree, another woman with long black hair and familiar eyes that Beth couldn't place, and Connor. It was titled, "The Dingle Contingent, Cambridge." Bram, Bree, Connor, and the woman, Alyson, were all tagged. Their young faces shone with excitement.

Her eyes lingered on his beautiful twenty-something face. His hair was longer, a wild mop of light brown. He was so familiar to her, it made her heart ache.

She scrolled back up and, like a true stalker, riffled through his friend drawer. The number of gorgeous women listed amongst his two thousand friends astounded her. She felt nauseated as she continued to scroll down the list of beautiful women and handsome men. She stopped once she got to a princess—perhaps the one the tabloids had mentioned. Elizabeth examined the unique gray eyes and perfect complexion of the princess, her hair curled elegantly in waves, her lips of ruby red. She looked straight out of a storybook.

Elizabeth quickly shut her laptop and shoved it to the side. She was thoroughly disgusted with herself for looking, thoroughly disgusted by her jealousy, and thoroughly disgusted that she had judged the situation so poorly.

They weren't even Facebook friends . . . how could she have been such a fool?

She reached for her phone, set an alarm, and closed her eyes. Hoping she would be able to evoke a case of selective amnesia once she woke, she drifted off into a dreamless sleep.

Chapter 12: The Ball

Elizabeth examined herself in the mirror. The Reem Acra was exquisite. Her hair was swept up in an intricate design.

Her makeup was light, except around the eyes. It was a marriage between a model and a fairy, and made her look like a cross between the two.

She didn't recognize herself. And yet, as she got closer to the mirror and studied her face, she saw someone there she'd only caught glimpses of in the last few months.

Her twenty-one-year-old vibrant self, the person she'd lost, the person Mags had been so proud of, was finally shining through.

She let out a sigh of sheer relief. Her mouth turned up into a joyous smile as she stared at herself. Thank God.

She'd woken to find her momentary nose-dive into the darkness was but a blip in her memory. A momentary lapse that wasn't a true barometer of her state of mind. It was a huge relief. She'd patched up the fissure in her chest with happy thoughts and could barely feel the scar as she recognized her old self in the mirror.

The doorbell rang. She grabbed her blue clutch and her phone from the bathroom counter as she left.

The ladies who'd helped her get ready reached the door and let Wes in. He was standing in the foyer like before, waiting.

Elizabeth reached the top of the stairs and looked down at him. His mouth dropped open; his eyes burned with intensity. His features finally settled.

He was giving her a look of total adoration.

The pleasant pink color started to rise, and her breathing shortened as she registered his expression.

She took one step at a time, careful to use the banister. Her five-inch heels clicked like the slow moving tick of a clock on the stairs.

The way he was looking at her. . . .

In an instant, she could see it all. See the way the night would go. Dancing under chandeliers. Light touches. Dark looks. A kiss.

And where it would end.

Wes gathering her in his arms . . . undressing her . . . taking her back upstairs. . . .

If she wanted it.

Her body felt warm as she imagined the night. Her life could go in so many different directions. Her skin tingled. The possibility excited her.

Suddenly, her cell buzzed in her hand, snapping her out of the daydream and demanding her attention.

A text.

I NEED TO SEE YOU LARA. PLEASE.

All the air left her lungs. And then another text.

I WILL SEE YOU TONIGHT EVEN IF I HAVE TO BREAK DOWN YOUR DOOR!

CONNOR.

Her stomach fell to her feet. The blood left her face.

His plea.

His threat.

She was angry. And something else. Something she wouldn't admit. Couldn't admit. Her heart fluttered; the color returned to her face all at once. The blood pooled lower.

She felt feverish.

Because she was angry.

Because he had no right.

She repeated the two thoughts like a single mantra, trying to convince herself that it was that simple.

That black and white.

Because how could it not be? All she'd ever expected from him was honesty. And in the end, a bloody tabloid had shown her the truth.

She didn't notice Wes, taking the steps three at a time to meet her.

"Liz, what's happened? What is it?" He took her hand and squeezed.

"No, it's nothing." Her voice shook, and then she regained herself. "I was just—just hoping to hear from Barry, the PI I hired, but it was nothing. Just Audre."

His eyes were still wide, unconvinced.

"That's right, I haven't told you about the show." She smiled bright, hoping it touched her eyes.

She crafted the cover lie well. Explaining how Audre had submitted her photograph. How it had been chosen and about the Wednesday judging and Saturday gala.

His answering smile was at once pleased for her and weary. "And that was it? Your face—you looked *ill*."

"Yeah, I guess I'm just a bit nervous, you know? My photo will be on a wall in the Natural History Museum . . . in London! *Being judged*." She shrugged like admitting her anxiety cost her something. Made her vulnerable somehow.

It didn't.

She was playing a part. Maneuvering her way through a situation, like an expert. An expert at manipulation.

Just like she used to.

Her tactics as an attorney were far more nuanced than raising her voice at opposing counsel or winning an argument merely through logic.

She manipulated the other person. Gave just the right smile. The right shrug. Appeared to show her cards, to show a vulnerability, when in fact she was just leading them to slaughter.

In that moment of recognition, she hated herself a little bit.

Despised how she could slip back into that mode of being so easily.

But her smile held. She radiated sincerity.

And he believed her. As she knew he would. For as much as she disliked herself for doing it, there was no way she was going to tell Wes about Connor's text.

She wouldn't allow his words to enter her world tonight.

The direction of the wind was clear.

Wasn't it?

Wes wrapped an arm around her waist and half-carried her down the stairs. Her feet barely touched the steps.

He set her down at the bottom. "You're the most beautiful creature I've ever laid eyes on." He kissed her cheek.

She walked towards the door, leaving him behind. "I bet you say that to all the girls," she teased over her shoulder. Her fingers reached the handle.

His British accent and altered cadence took her back to a different time. "I can assure you, I've never uttered those words in my life," he whispered from behind her.

After walking the red carpet set opposite the Thames, Wes had ushered her through a side entrance where they were able to go through security more quickly.

The Grand Hall in Old Billingsgate was magnificent. The hall was at least six times the size of Wilton's. It had tall pillars and a triple-height vaulted ceiling made of glass.

A complicated black rigging system was set up to provide dramatic chandelier spotlights.

Then there were the thousands of additional lights that dripped from the rig. Like white icicle lights at Christmas, only these strings were much longer and reminded her of the leaves of a willow tree—if they were made of light.

Four pillar candles that measured between two and three feet tall served as centerpieces on the round white linen-covered tables that seated ten. Elegant satin silk fabric covered the plush chairs as well.

A very large part of the space was reserved for the dance floor.

"We're at capacity with one thousand," Wes explained as he showed her to their table in the center, just off the dance floor.

"Every year, I find myself turning more benefactors away—always with a gentle nudge to send donations directly to my office or through the website, of course."

"Naturally." Beth smiled back, amused that he looked so proud of his efforts. Justifiably proud, but a youthful proud—like a boy who can't quite believe he'd managed to scale a tall mountain.

"This year we sold out in an hour." He beamed.

There were at least five hundred people there already, buzzing about and doing the elegant kiss-on-both-cheeks greeting. They glittered and gleamed in tuxedos and couture gowns—some, no doubt, specially made for the occasion.

He looked down at her, then with a glint in his eyes, said, "Did I mention Her Majesty, the Queen will make an appearance after dinner?"

She pursed her lips, attempting to hide her smile. "No, you failed to mention that." She narrowed her eyes at him, now clearly able to see that he'd failed to mention it on purpose, perhaps to shock and impress her at that very moment.

"Audre filled me in last night," she said, letting the annoyance color her voice.

"Oh, come now." He laughed and wrapped an arm around her until she was flush against him. "Don't be angry with me. It was just a bit of fun. I'll introduce you if you like." His eyes were nothing but mischief.

Wes was likely to say something odd to embarrass her in front of the Queen. Nothing too grievous, just something like, *Elizabeth enjoys breaking into Kensington Gardens, Your Majesty, and playing with the Peter Pan statue.*

He'd get a good laugh and she'd get him back later, but the experience was to be avoided.

"That's OK." She placed a hand on his chest, registering how strong his arms felt around her, how it might feel to have her skin pressed against his.

She flushed, trying to push the thought away. "I intended to study after dinner last night, and then today but the time just got away from me. I'd have no idea what to do or say."

He smiled, holding on to her more tightly. "You don't have to say anything, really—just curtsy and take a photo."

"Still, if it's just the same to you, I'd like to keep this night in the fashionably elegant category and not venture into the over-the-top *holy crap I'm meeting the Queen* category."

He shrugged, which allowed her to feel his muscles ripple against her. "Suit yourself."

Just then a young man approached and Wes released her.

The man said something to him quietly and Wes excused himself to go deal with the issue.

For the next twenty minutes, Beth wandered around the room, up the stairs to the mezzanine, and out to the riverside terrace that overlooked the Thames and Tower Bridge.

She made small talk with random people as she stood examining the pieces created by the young artists that Wes' organization, Angels of Young Artists, or AYA for short, supported.

It was pleasant conversation with the young and the old. Beth commended each guest for showing their support and making such an impact on young lives.

Everything that came out of her mouth was genuine, but she felt at times like a hostess, promoting her husband's work, promoting the cause.

Some of the guests asked her about her connection to AYA. Every time Beth mentioned Wes, people looked at her with a new sense of respect, of importance . . . of *awe*.

It was odd.

And yet, the exchanges helped her to understand just how well-regarded Wes had come to be in London. For the first time, she felt the honor of his having asked her to come with him.

Wes stood to give a short speech after dinner. The thousand guests became so silent, you could hear a whisper.

He thanked everyone for their support and even made a point to thank his beautiful date, Elizabeth—many eyes had turned to her at that point. It was the type of attention Beth shied away from. But she flushed and smiled pleasantly, trying to look composed.

Then there was the five-minute documentary that chronicled AYA's impact on three artists over the last five years. One had gone on to exhibit at a posh gallery when he turned eighteen, another went to study art in the U.S., and the third was making a living by selling her art online—enough to buy her mother a house in a better neighborhood.

It was a beautiful video that, among other things, made Beth feel slightly inadequate. Here was her gorgeous goofball friend, Wes, making a difference and changing lives, while she'd been off lining her pockets by helping people get divorced.

Wes could do whatever he wanted. He never had to make a living, she reminded herself, fighting that judgmental part of her brain that sometimes came out to punish her for the choices she'd made.

She forced herself to focus, standing with everyone else as they clapped after the video and Wes' speech. He walked across the dance floor, all masculine authority.

People were still on their feet when he reached her. His eyes hooded over as he caught sight of something behind her. Then, very deliberately, he smiled his gorgeous smile and brought her into his arms, breaking away from her just long enough to kiss her thoroughly on the lips.

It threw her.

Wes had never been the type to shy away from public displays of affection, but this was shocking even for him. Her skin felt hot as she thought about all the eyes still on them.

Finally, he released her and she sank back into her chair, stunned. Desperately trying to regain her composure.

Completely untroubled, he took his seat next to her.

The murmurs of the crowd continued as they did the same, sitting down to their dessert.

People were giving her sidelong glances. Some looked shocked, others smiled, and yet others wore expressions of awe that matched the looks she'd received earlier when she'd mentioned Wes.

She narrowed her eyes, wanting to lay into him, but she knew doing so would only give people more to gossip about.

And he looked so happy.

Happy that he'd kissed her in front of everyone and pleased the presentation had been so well received.

If she hadn't been so embarrassed, she would have thought his look was endearing.

She resolved to bring it up later, when they weren't surrounded by curious eyes.

The champagne and dessert went a long way to make her forget her embarrassment. Sugar and booze had that effect on her.

Even so, Wes kept giving her worried looks when he thought she couldn't see. He knew her well and could read through her composed expression, to what lay beneath.

She sipped her champagne and looked away from him, pretending not to notice his concern.

Just then the music swelled. A string quartet had set up at the top of the floor, near where Wes had given his speech.

Wes stood and extended a hand to her, an invitation to dance. She pursed her lips, seeing through the gesture. His eyes were already dancing mischievously, daring her to turn him down in front of everyone.

He wasn't playing fair. Sugar, booze, and dancing— the trifecta. All unpleasantness could be erased by this most holy of trinities.

She'd just placed her hand in his to accept, when Winston apparated beside Wes.

"Hello, Cartwright, excellent speech!" Winston clapped a hand on his shoulder.

Beth stood to shake his hand politely.

"Yes, thank you for your support." Wes gave Winston a nod, and then placed an arm around Beth's waist.

"Elizabeth Lara, meet Lord Walter Betheny, Earl of Chittenden."

"Hello again," Beth said brightly.

"What a pleasure to see you again, my dear." He gave her a courtly nod. "This is quite the to-do I mentioned, is it not?"

"Yes, it is a spectacular evening," she agreed.

The same young man from earlier whispered something quietly to Wes, who then released her.

With an excited smile, he said, "Please excuse me, I have some business to attend to." He gave Walter a nod and then threw Beth a knowing look of warning.

She understood.

As soon as Wes was gone, Beth excused herself politely to visit the loo. She even used the word "loo" and thought, for a moment, that her voice took on a British accent.

She was sure it came out sounding more Bridget Jones and less Duchess of Cambridge.

After she'd inspected herself in the mirror for an appropriate amount of time, she emerged back into the main hall.

There were more men in black suits with earpieces than before. In fact, she'd barely noticed them earlier. Now they seemed to be everywhere.

She looked back towards her table. Wes was nowhere to be seen, but Lord Walter was still standing at the table, chatting with someone she'd never met. He was searching the room for someone as he talked, making no effort to look interested in what the other man was saying.

Whether he was actually looking for Beth, she'd never know, because when Walter's head turned in her direction she quickly ducked behind a group of people standing to the side of the room, near one of the grand pillars.

She was still concealing herself behind the group, in a manner befitting of a Meg Ryan film, when someone moved past, knocking her off-balance. She stepped forward into the group to steady herself, only to realize it was moving forward into the next room.

She tried to get out of the way, but found she couldn't pay attention to where the line was going and shield herself from Walter at the same time.

After a minute, she could see that he'd asked someone to dance and was finally preoccupied by a lovely woman in her forties.

Beth let out an audible sigh, at once registering the people giving her strange looks all around her. They were waiting for her to step forward. A kind-looking man in his sixties held out a hand, beckoning her to step in front of him.

"Thank you," she said automatically, not sure why he'd made the gesture.

Hesitantly, she stepped in front of him. The next thing she knew, a man had grabbed her by the elbow gently and ushered her into the next room, until she was standing in front of a petite woman in blue.

Beth froze, recognizing her immediately.

Holy. . . ! What had Wes said? Curtsy. . . ?

Beth placed the ball of her foot behind the heel of the other, her arms to the side, and bent her knees. It was an awkward sort of curtsy. But the only one even the most graceful of women could have managed in five-inch heels.

The man led her forward.

The room was filled with security and bright studio lighting. An elegantly-dressed photographer stood at the center of the room, opposite the woman in blue.

How was this happening?

The man who'd ushered her in placed her next to the woman.

Beth tried to take deep breaths through her fixed smile, but felt a nervous sort of panic coming on.

"Yes, just there," the photographer instructed, as his assistant moved her an inch to her right. And again.

Elizabeth went reluctantly, feeling like an awkward teenager who'd missed the day on royal etiquette.

Why hadn't she studied? It was the same sinking feeling of taking a pop quiz when you didn't know any of the answers.

The tall, balding man in the elegant dark suit behind the camera continued, "Make haste, Dorren."

The assistant named Dorren closed the distance between Elizabeth and the tiny woman next to her. Another Elizabeth.

Beth smiled nervously at her; Dorren's placement had brought her close enough to feel the woman's blue silk dress. The silver-haired lady smiled up at her kindly. The diamonds on her head caught the light from the elegant chandelier above.

"Lovely, we're there. On three. One . . . two. . . ." Beth turned to the camera. She held her smile, trying not to look disbelieving. "Three." The shutter clicked. "Thank you, Your Majesty."

With a wave of his hand, the photographer instructed Dorren to bring in the next group.

CHAPTER 13: AN UNEXPECTED DANCE

Elizabeth was ushered out of the room and back out to the hall again.

She was so dazed by the encounter that she hardly noticed where she was going and nearly bumped into several people as she made her way back to her seat.

A combination of "I'm so sorry!" and "Please excuse me!" got her safely back to her table. She was just about to sit down when Lord Walter apparated like before.

"Theeere you are, my dear. You missed the grand entrance! Her Majesty, the Queen has arrived!" He spoke animatedly. "I'd be happy to provide an introduction as I see that Cartwright continues to be otherwise engaged."

Walter moved his head this way and that, as if trying to locate Wes. It was a vacant gesture.

"Thank you, but I've just had the pleasure." Beth found her voice, tapping in to her experience in the courtroom. The wits she'd called on when it had become necessary to recover quickly from an answer she wasn't expecting in cross.

He took a step closer to her, and then another, until he was far too close for comfort. He was good-looking, but the proximity was starting to make her skin crawl.

Wes was right. *Definitely a cad.*

"Oh, well, perhaps you'll join me for a drink on the terrace. There is the most breathtaking view of Tower Bridge—"

"Thank you," she cut him off and stepped back decisively. "But I've already seen it."

Whether it was the drink or his natural personality, it appeared that Lord Walter could not take a hint.

"Really." She stepped back and then realized that she had nowhere to go. She dropped her clutch on the table. Her hands were pinned behind her, on the other side of the chair; she tried to see a way to maneuver away from him.

She didn't want to make a scene for Wes' sake. But this man needed handling. . . .

Just then a hand interlaced with her fingers from behind and brought her arm around to the front and then out to the side. The hand pulled her past Walter in one brisk movement.

The earl barely had time to move out of the way as she was whisked onto the dance floor and straight into a waltz.

Beth looked gratefully into the face of her rescuer as they turned smoothly to the music, but then her heart fell to her feet and the blood rose to her face.

Instead of seeing eyes of green-gray, they were eyes of ice blue.

She was waltzing around the room in Connor's arms.

"What the—" She was dumbfounded.

"Lara," was his simple answer.

He gave her his most dazzling smile. The one that looked like Christmas morning, nothing at all the matter. Like it was the most natural thing in the world for him to be dancing with her, here at Wes' event.

"What are you doing here?" she whispered so that none of the other couples could hear the alarm in her voice.

She looked around to see if anyone had noticed how closely he was holding her, especially since she'd just been seen kissing Wes.

She tried to push away from him. But he expected it and used his strength to keep her firmly in place.

"You look beautiful." He ignored her.

Her eyes were wide, but she fixed a smile on her face so that she wouldn't call any attention to them. "Seriously, Bannon, what . . . are . . . you doing here?" she said through gritted teeth.

"I came to dance with you." He still sounded so completely unaffected that it made Beth seethe.

Suddenly struck by the urge she'd been keeping at bay for the better part of a week, she pressed her thumb into his upper arm, squeezing a pressure point.

He winced.

Still smiling and speaking through gritted teeth, she continued. "Seriously, if you don't stop talking to me like there's nothing wrong with this and start making sense, I'm going to skewer your foot with the spike of my heel and make it look like an accident."

She smiled pleasantly, nodding to the other couples, before continuing. "Then I'm going to help you off the dance floor, blame it on my being such a klutz, shove you into a chair and leave you there."

His lips pressed together as he tried to breathe through the pain shooting up his arm from her grip.

"Got it?" she asked.

He smiled, jaw clenched tight. "Yes."

She released the pressure.

"Now, what are you doing here? How did you even get in? And why are you just showing up like this?"

He tried to lighten the mood, "Should I answer in that specific order, or. . . ?"

She stared daggers at him.

"OK. I came to see you. When I realized where he must be taking you, I used my connections to get a ticket at the last minute. And I'm showing up because . . . *I missed you.*" His eyes were earnest.

Something in her chest tightened. She looked away. "Don't do this, Connor."

"Do what, Luv? Be honest?"

Was he serious?

She gave him a hard sort of laugh.

He could hear all that she wouldn't say in it.

"Why won't you talk to me, Lara?"

She avoided his eyes.

His voice grew soft. "What changed since that day outside of the cottage?"

"You can't possibly be this thick," she answered under her breath.

"I thought—" he started, voice full of pain, "I thought that I'd come back and we might be able to . . . start again?" He shook his head, like he was trying to understand why she was choosing to hurt him.

Why was *he* pained?

What was wrong with this man?

She'd already mentioned the tabloid and how informative it had been. Was he really so daft that he hadn't understood her meaning two days ago?

No, she'd mentioned the picture. *It said a thousand words,* she'd told him.

He knew and yet he was choosing to ignore it.

Why? For what possible purpose?

Did he think he could just bat his eyes at her? A few *Lara*s and hungry eyes, and she'd be good to go?

She'd been clear before about honesty. After he'd kept his title from her . . . she wouldn't give him another opportunity to explain.

He was searching her face, willing her to say something.

She dropped the anger.

She wanted answers, and it wouldn't serve her in this particular conversation. "What do you want from me,

Connor? What are you looking for exactly, because I honestly don't know which way is up with you."

Half of her response was a manipulation to get answers, and the other half was just Beth.

He drew his eyebrows together. "I want you, Lara. What do I have to say, what do I have to do to get you to talk to me?"

"Is that what you want? To talk?" She shook her head. "OK, then, *talk*."

She bit the inside of her lip so she could listen to him without letting all of her emotions show on her face.

He looked around. "Not here. If I could just come by. Maybe later tonight?"

"What's wrong with right here?"

"You have your walls up. You won't listen here."

Her eyes flashed with anger. "What's there to even listen to?"

Was he deaf?

She wanted to yell, "*Go back to your supermodel!*" But it didn't seem likely that the outburst would be well received.

"There are many things to say," he said pointedly.

"I'm all ears." She tried and failed to keep the sarcasm out of her voice.

"No, you're not." His accent was thick, Irish.

"You want to talk, but you aren't *saying* anything," she spit at him through gritted teeth, still holding the smile.

This was exhausting. It was like they were speaking two different languages.

He wanted to talk, this was his opportunity, but he refused to say anything that mattered.

Not that he could say anything that *would* make a difference.

She dropped the façade. "Connor, it's fine. There's nothing to talk about. We parted ways that day in front of Rhia's cottage. Our story was lovely, but it was meant to be brief. You moved on. I moved on. It's really all right. It just is what it is." She shrugged in his arms.

"Please stop showing up and saying that you want to talk and then refusing to really say anything at all."

She let the exhaustion into her voice, let him hear it so he would understand. So he would leave her alone.

He stared deeply into her eyes, trying desperately to convey something. "It's been six weeks. I thought about you all the time—didn't you think about me?"

Beth kept silent. She didn't want to let it all out.

"I wrote things down. Things I wanted to tell you about," he continued.

Some of what she was feeling slipped out in spite of herself. The smile vanished; the whisper was scathing. "If you spent all this time thinking about me, then why were you in Paris for an entire week before you showed up at my door? And how you knew exactly where I was living is another question I'd like answered—and how you got my number, for that matter."

She purposely left out the supermodel. The kiss.

He shook his head impatiently. "It doesn't matter. I'll tell you everything, just . . . tell me that you care."

"I did care, Connor. I was never anything but honest with you. But like I said, we had our ending."

His eyes were fierce, his words forceful. "No, tell me that you care. *Now*. Today."

His voice went silky smooth; it sent desire shooting through her. "Here." He brought his lips to her ear and whispered, "In my arms."

He held her closer.

"I'm here with Wes," she said firmly, not trusting herself to answer the question he'd asked.

He snapped back. His accent was thick, Irish. "Yes, I saw with my own two eyes how *with* Wes y'are," he said angrily, turning faster than the tempo of the waltz allowed, almost colliding with another couple.

"Jaysus, woman, you're tearing my guts out!"

Her eyes shot to his instinctively. How could they not with that admission?

The look of anguish on his face pierced her heart. For a moment she wanted to touch him, soothe him, take away the pain.

But the memory of the blonde's arms wrapped around his neck slapped her back to reality.

Her eyes flashed and her voice dripped with disdain. "That's not what it looked like a week ago!"

He recoiled and then something else touched his eyes . . . *satisfaction? Hope?*

170

She shook her head; it was pointless to guess what he was thinking.

"If you're talking about Sade, then don't believe everything you see in the tabloids. After the last few months, I thought if anyone had learned that lesson it would be you."

His words stung. Hearing him even say the blonde's name made her feel a little sick, and the dig about the rags in Ireland didn't help.

Although they had gotten a lot wrong, there was truth at the heart of *that* story.

And the pictures of *them* kissing at the town hall in Dingle were real. . . .

She looked away from him as the blood drained down to her toes.

He read her face and softened. "You really are a vision. My heart stopped when I first saw you."

Her eyes took him in for the first time; he looked beautiful in his tuxedo. His light brown hair was longer, with bits of red she'd never noticed.

For a fraction of a second she allowed herself to remember him lying in bed. Arm supporting his head, the white sheet coming up just below his hips. Her favorite picture of him.

And she felt the familiar pull, the desire to feel his skin, his body.

And then, fittingly, the music stopped.

And the world stopped spinning with it.

Someone tapped Connor on the shoulder. They both turned to find Wes, his jaw set in a line. "May I cut in." It wasn't a question.

Connor's back straightened a degree. The veins in his temples popped.

His muscles flexed, probably involuntarily.

The alpha male in him rose to meet the alpha male in Wes. It was an odd exchange to have on a dance floor surrounded by women in ball gowns and men in tuxedos, dainty strings playing in the background.

Reluctantly, Connor released Beth and stepped aside.

Wes took her into his arms, pressing their hips together and setting their frame. The song wasn't a regular waltz, it was a Viennese—the typical waltz everyone associated with elegant balls.

"Is everything all right?" he asked as the world turned twice as fast as before.

Though their hips were connected, the dance frame required her to look up and out, arching her back away from him, keeping only her lower ribs connected to his torso.

"Fine; I was just surprised to see him here." She was a bit winded from the dance.

"Yes, I don't know how he got in." He was grim.

"He said he used his connections."

His voice was strained. "Ah, I forgot how well connected the wanker can be."

As Wes spun her around the floor, she caught glimpses of Connor first standing at her table and then leaning against a pillar on the edge of the floor. His arms were crossed, his expression bleak.

Some part of her took pleasure in seeing him so affected by Wes.

Halfway through the dance, a woman in her twenties approached Connor. She was petite, perky, and pretty.

She kept talking to him while he watched Beth dancing. For the most part he ignored her, until she touched his arm flirtatiously.

Beth flushed. That sick, jealous feeling began to set in again. It was a relief to pass through the part of the dance floor that allowed her to see what was going on. She saw him move away from the woman's touch.

The corners of her mouth twitched up. Beth felt more pleased than was probably healthy.

Connor looked up just then and caught her staring at him. His eyes flashed, glinted with that same look he'd worn before . . . satisfaction?

His lips twitched up in response, but his eyes . . . they turned hungry.

She forced herself to look away the next time she passed.

When the song ended, Beth found herself taking a few covert glances around the room. Connor was nowhere in sight. She wouldn't see him again at the AYA Ball.

Without his eyes on her, she felt more relaxed, and she and Wes settled into an easy rhythm. There was no event crisis to pull him away from her again.

They spent the rest of the night dancing and laughing and talking.

Wes didn't ask her about Connor until they were in the car.

She'd been distracted, looking out at the city through the window, saying nothing.

"Eh . . . what did you and Bannon talk about?"

The question threw her. From his tone she could tell he had been building up to asking. She'd thought they were riding in comfortable silence, pleasantly content from their night of revelry.

Without looking from the window, she replied, "We talked about talking." It was the truth.

"Sorry, I don't follow."

She turned to him. "I didn't either. He wanted to talk to me, refused to talk during the dance, and said not to believe everything I see in the tabloids."

"Is this about him and that supermodel?"

She raised an eyebrow, surprised he knew.

He tilted his head. "This is England. The tabloids are inescapable."

She nodded. "I guess. I didn't bring it up. I told him that we'd both moved on and that it was fine. There was nothing left to talk about."

"Did he deny that it was him in the photos?"

"No." She turned back to the window. "It's fine. I just wish he would stop showing up like that."

And then she remembered something. "Although, his timing tonight may have saved your event from ending up in the rags tomorrow."

Her smile was all mischief.

He narrowed his eyes, trying to guess her game. "Is that so? Please, tell me how I owe this *narrow* escape to Connor Bannon?"

"Walter had me cornered—like literally cornered against the table. I was trying to work out how to maneuver myself around him so that the bastard couldn't touch me. He was close . . . and I was close to, you know, *retaliating*—I mean *defending* myself. How has that man not been charged with something by now?"

Wes' jaw clenched. He shook his head, completely disgusted with Walter. "Unfathomable. Even knowing that you were very much there with me, he still. . . ."

He couldn't finish.

She laughed, trying to lighten the mood. "Anyway, that's when Connor . . . uh, grabbed my hand and led me to the floor. Walter barely had time to move out of the way."

Her voice was light, but it did nothing to lighten Wes' features. His face just grew darker. She stopped smiling abruptly. "Guess you had to be there. . . ." She trailed off and turned her attention back to the window.

"If Bannon hadn't been caught with Sade, would you be dating him right now?"

She thought through this as best she could. "Honestly, I don't know. We said goodbye in Ireland. We didn't have any plans to see each other or reconnect. He didn't even know where or how to reach me—"

"He found you regardless," Wes said under his breath.

She ignored him. "As I said, we had no plans to meet. I made it very clear to him that I had my own journey to follow and it didn't line up with his in Africa—so I really don't know."

Beth sighed. "The tabloid was just a visual confirmation of what had been technically true for six weeks—that it was over."

She tried to sound matter-of-fact, but some sadness crept in.

Wes examined her face. "Thank you for being honest."

She shrugged. "It's what I do." *Most of the time*, she thought.

He reached over to lace his fingers through hers, appeased by her answer.

Chapter 14: Lighter Fluid & Puccini

It was nearly three in the morning, but Beth was still wired from the dancing, and the Queen, and the gorgeous men.

She changed into a blush tank top and white sleep shorts, but didn't touch her hair or makeup. She would save *that* ordeal for later.

Downstairs, she poured herself a glass of sauvignon blanc, grabbed a box of chocolates she'd picked up while shopping for her dress, and settled into the reading nook, thinking about Wes' goodnight kiss.

With no one to interrupt, their embrace had ended with him pinning her against the door. She'd almost considered letting him in.

Almost.

She smiled and sipped her wine happily as she read random articles off the GoodNewsNetwork.

There was a woman, Beth Moon, who'd spent fourteen years photographing ancient trees. From the U.S. to Africa, the portraits were hauntingly beautiful.

She bit into an orange chocolate truffle as she read about the RAKNomination movement which was sweeping the UK and Europe. People filmed themselves performing random acts of kindness and then used social media to challenge two or more friends to do the same.

After picking another chocolate, a mystery confection with sprinkles, she ventured onto YouTube, finding old videos of Improv Everywhere.

She laughed hysterically at the "No Pants Subway Ride" videos and re-watched some of her favorites, like the prank where everyone froze in Grand Central Station.

Beth continued merrily in this way with her wine and her comedy and her chocolate until she heard a tapping noise. Like something hitting glass.

She paused the video and listened. There it was again.

It wasn't very loud, and it wasn't following any discernible rhythm.

She stilled.

Tap.

It was coming from the window.

And again.

Someone was throwing something at No. 3.

Sitting at the window seat in the nook, she looked down but couldn't see anything. Cautiously, she stepped onto the terrace and looked over the side.

Connor, still in his tuxedo, was standing just inside the gate throwing pebbles at her window.

It was such a strange sight and she was in such a good mood that any annoyance she might have felt an hour before was notably absent.

Beth leaned on the railing of the terrace with her elbows.

She couldn't keep a straight face. "Is this—" She chuckled. "is this the part where," she laughed again, "where I'm supposed to say '*Romeo, Romeo*?'" She couldn't hold it in. She laughed so hard she wasn't sure she hadn't woken the neighbors.

She covered her mouth with her hand, which only made her snort and then laugh harder.

"Lara," Connor whispered up, "will you please let me in? Your neighbor next door is giving me a very stern look through his window." He pointed at No. 4.

She had stopped laughing, but little fits of odd-sounding giggles still bubbled up between words. She was thinking of John Cusack. "Where's your boom box?"

And then she burst out again, holding her stomach as she doubled over. Nothing could be funnier to Beth, especially after wine and chocolate, than a good old-fashioned eighties reference.

The lights at No. 5 went on. Oh, now she'd done it. She stopped and whispered down to him, "You're just going to keep showing up, aren't you?"

"You bet your bottom I am," he whispered back.

She'd have to let him in or risk waking more of the neighbors. And the wealthy Londoners who called Rose Square home could be a cranky bunch.

Without saying anything else, she went downstairs and let him in.

He followed her up the steps and into the living area.

"Would you like a glass of wine?" She made her way to the kitchen, not waiting for an answer.

"Er. . . ."

She handed him the glass without looking at him and walked to the large ivory couch opposite the Chagall.

She folded her feet underneath her and extended an arm along the top of the couch. The other held her glass.

She waited.

He came to sit on the other end, angling towards her.

Her good mood would not be tarnished. It was up to him where this went. Her mind was clear of all expectations, the good and the bad.

"So. . . ." he began, his accent thick.

She waited.

"Where to begin," he mused.

She tilted her head.

And waited.

"Thank you for seeing me." He was formal.

Like she had a choice.

He took a sip of his wine. And then a swig.

Apparently, her silence was making him nervous.

She was trying not to care, but it was difficult. She enjoyed affecting him like this.

He cleared his throat. "Can I ask you something?" All hesitancy was gone.

"You can ask, but I may not answer."

"Fair enough. If you do answer, though, let it be the whole truth. No walls." The intensity of his gaze made her mouth go dry.

It felt like he was trying to communicate something. The importance of this moment, of her answer.

A choice was to be made. She could sense it. Her heart began to thump more loudly in her ears. A fork in the road. *Two roads diverged in a yellow wood. . . .*

She'd always been able to sense these moments, even as she'd given herself over to the law. Surrendered to the dark. She knew it then.

It felt like ten years had been taken from her. Stolen. But it was only partly true. She'd stood at that precipice and chosen her path. She couldn't know the extent of the darkness then, or where it would end, but she'd known she was choosing it.

She swallowed. Goose bumps had formed on her skin. What would she choose now?

"Go on," she prodded.

He studied her face, carefully examining every micro-expression as she waited for him to ask his question. "What did you feel when you saw the photo of me and Sade?"

She hated hearing him refer to it, even now. Hated seeing the name come out of his mouth.

She shook her head. "Let's not do this, Connor. Please."

With a shrug, she tried to sidestep. "None of it matters anymore. I'd like to think back on what we had and remember the way we were without thinking on . . . the rest. Can't you allow me that?" She narrowed her eyes.

Why was he so determined to make her talk about this? Did he take some secret pleasure in tormenting her?

"No, Lara. It does matter. That's what I'm sayin'. It *does* matter. Please, just tell me what you felt."

The bile rose to her throat as she thought about being sucker-punched in the middle of the street . . . after she'd just been on some stupid, naive cloud nine seconds before.

In that moment she hated him.

Loathed the sight of him.

How could she have thought this man was a stand-up guy? Who *does* this? Goes out of his way to poke and prod someone just to see what happens?

"Tell me, Elizabeth." He was more forceful now, his voice rising. She tried not to look at him. She couldn't look at him. But he just kept coming at her. Forcing the issue. "What. Did. YOU. FEEL?!"

He grabbed her hand.

Who the hell did he think he was?

She yanked it away and stood up, placing her glass on the coffee table.

She paced the floor between the couches and the kitchen, hands on her hips, breathing deeply.

Trying to calm herself, needing to calm herself. If she didn't, she might lose it. And it wouldn't be pretty.

It was the closest to outright violence she'd ever been.

He stood, walking towards her.

No, no, no.

She raised a hand out to stop him from touching her. Her eyes flashed with a fire that bolted him to the ground.

Even his face stilled, until something bubbled up. A fire that rose up in him, daring him to keep going, keep pressing the issue.

She gave him a look of warning, pressing her lips together so hard and holding so much tension in her face that it hurt.

But Connor had come here for a reason. He had a plan and he would see it through. His body was ramrod straight, rigid with the tension and the fight he knew he was about to provoke. He took one last breath.

And then, the choice.

"WHAT DID YOU FEEL?!" He hurled the words at her. It was like lighting a match. He'd already placed the gunpowder barrels next to each other and drenched them in lighter fluid.

Elizabeth stood facing him, her hands balled into fists.

And then she couldn't hold on anymore.

"I FELT SICK, YOU BLOODY BASTARD!" Her entire body vibrated with the intensity of it. The words were bigger than her five-foot-four frame. She stood on her tiptoes, angling her body forward, willing her words to hit him, so she wouldn't close the easy distance and punch him in the face.

"WHAT THE HELL DO YOU WANT FROM ME?! WHAT IS THIS, SOME SICK GAME?!" She narrowed her eyes, wanting to hurt him, but not knowing how.

"I FELT LIKE I'D BEEN SUCKER-PUNCHED IN THE MIDDLE OF THE STREET!"

At this, Connor's body relaxed. His shoulders fell; his lungs filled with the air he hadn't even realized he was missing. His face smoothed.

And then he gave her his dazzling smile. It was exactly what he'd needed to hear.

Elizabeth came off of her tiptoes and took a step back. Her features drew together in anger and confusion. He really took pleasure in this. It had been the only logical conclusion she'd been able to come to, but seeing him smile at her seemed to confirm that most impossible of conclusions.

The Connor she knew could not have taken pleasure in her pain.

He held up his hands in surrender. "Lara." It was a gentle caress, a vow. All severity had vanished.

He took a step towards her.

She took a step away from him.

What was he playing at? Her anger dissipated a degree as the confusion started to gain ground.

No, he couldn't be this malicious. It wasn't right.

Her brain continued to analyze the situation, think through every piece like a puzzle. It didn't fit. The logic didn't fit. He wasn't making any sense.

And because the anger had made her body so ripe with tension and anxiety that she was now in physical pain, she let her brain carry her further and further away from it.

He dropped his hands to his side. Cautiously now, he motioned to the couch. "Come back and sit down." His eyes pleaded with her. "I'll tell you everything."

She went, if only to reconnect with her wine, willing it to soothe her. She took up her glass and her position on the couch, waiting.

"Would it be better for you if you cross-examined me or if I just spoke?" he asked, taking his seat opposite her and removing his black tuxedo jacket. Ready to get into it.

She didn't trust herself to answer; instead, she sipped her wine, focusing on the dry fruit flavors. It went down her throat like a tonic.

"Right, I'll just jump in then. First, I came back a week earlier than expected for Sade."

Elizabeth downed the rest of her glass.

"No—not like that!" He held a hand out and then ran it through his hair. "Jaysus, I'm making a mess of things, aren't I?"

She just glared at him.

"I mean to say—that I came back because I'd heard about her and Chase breaking up and I was hoping to take a look at this rare ruby he'd given her—"

"Did you ask to see the stone and then just *magically* fall into her lucky charms?" She cut him off and rose to refill her glass, taking a chocolate from the box still on the window seat.

This situation required more chocolate.

When she'd returned to the couch, he continued. "I wanted to see if it matched a description I'd found related to my ancestors and maybe buy it for my auction house—but the stone isn't important." He waved a hand like he was trying to get himself back on track.

"I noticed the paps following us from the start—I'd taken her out to dinner to discuss possible terms of sale. Halfway through I came up with an idea. She was so miserable about Chase and I—I thought about you a lot in Africa, and about us. I knew I wanted to come back early. I knew I'd have to do something drastic to find out how you really felt.

"It was so easy, you see. For you to go off in your own direction without me. When I was alone, I questioned everything. So I made a decision. At the time, it seemed like a wise plan, a way to gauge how you felt, how deep your feelings ran."

She sat up, listening now.

"I told Sade of my plan, and about you, and she agreed. She wanted to get back at Chase—it was mutually beneficial. So I kissed her, knowing the pap was there and knowing that it would make the rags even in London because of the timing of Sade and Chase's breakup."

Her jaw dropped.

"So you see, there never was any Sade. Later, I wondered if I'd made the right decision. Agonized about it, really, especially knowing your temperament." He chuckled sadly and ran his fingers through his hair.

"But it always felt like I was all in, seeing a life with you—and you still kept your heart locked away. It felt like it hurt me much more than it hurt you when I left.

"I knew even then that I would pursue you in London, but our time apart made me question the depth of your feelings. It drove me mad at times, so when the thought came to me at that dinner, I had to see it through—to see if you cared for me the way I cared for you.

"If you didn't, you would keep being cool, unaffected. And you *were* that night outside when you were here with Cartwright." He spoke Wes' name like it was a curse word.

"You mentioned the photo, but you seemed little more than resigned to it, not upset or angry or passionate. I wanted you to feel hurt and a little mad—but it seemed to backfire since it was me who was gutted when I showed up at your door and found you with him. *I* was the one who felt those things and I resented you for it, so I acted the maggot.

"And then you wouldn't speak to me. I kept texting and leaving messages, but you wouldn't see me. I had to do something even if it seemed you weren't affected by the Sade photo—I couldn't leave you alone even if you didn't care as much as I did. So I paid an ungodly amount to attend Cartwright's event just to see you.

"When we danced and I told you that you were tearing my guts out, I thought there was a moment when you were on the edge of—but then your face changed again and you looked angry. You looked like you hated me and then you threw in that dig about what happened a week ago—and I knew you had to be talkin' about the photo—and that look of anger, there was passion in it, I thought for the first time . . . maybe. . . ?

"And then when I was watching you dance with *him*, that woman came up to me and started flirtin'. I caught your face—it was there, you . . . *didn't like it*. At first I thought I was hoping to see it on your face, but then I blew her off and you smiled. You tried to hide it, but you smiled, Lara.

"That's when I knew you still cared, knew you were hidin' behind that nasty concrete wall of yours—afraid to get hurt, too proud to look weak. So I knew I'd have to push your buttons until it forced you to smash the wall—even if it meant I had to blow it up.

"I had to draw out your anger so that I could draw out the truth. And not just for me, but for you. You weren't being honest with yourself—you're mad about me, Lara, admit it." He smiled, and let out a big gust of air. Relieved to finally rid himself of the truth.

To lay it at her feet.

It was clear from his expression that he was feeling rather pleased with himself.

Like it would all be OK now.

Grand, even.

The truth was out. There was no one but her.

She could return to Fantasyland effective immediately, complete with a dolphin *and* a castle.

Case closed. Cue Puccini. The big, boisterous notes of "Nessun Dorma" should start any minute now as they ride off into the sunset.

He didn't know her as well as he thought. Or women, for that matter.

She blinked, her expression vacant.

He waited.

She tried to wrap her brain around what he'd just said. *So he'd manipulated her.*

His smile started to fade with the tick of the old grandfather clock on the stairs.

His relief turned to concern. "Lara?"

She tilted her head and narrowed her eyes, trying to understand how he could possibly think it would all be OK now.

His voice wavered. "You understand . . . Sade and me, there was nothing between us. It was all an act for the cameras. I haven't seen anyone else. I haven't even *thought* of anyone else. Just you."

She opened her mouth, but nothing came out.

"We can be together now. I'm mad about you—the entire time I was traveling in Africa I wished you were there with me. I'm usually quite content on my solo acquisition trips, spend the months in between building a hankering for them even."

He reached for her hand and squeezed. His ice blue eyes burned with sincerity. "But this time I felt like I'd left half of myself behind. Do you understand what I'm sayin', Luv?"

She wasn't blind to his heartfelt confession.

The picture in the press had created a knot in the pit of her stomach—she hadn't noticed, but it had stayed with her since first she laid eyes on the blonde. But now it seemed to have disappeared. It *was* a relief.

But he was just so certain that they could pick up where they'd left off because he was mad about her and she was mad about him and that's all there was to it.

Was she mad about him?

Oh, the difference of a single week.

Connor still had a hold over her, but. . . .

She extracted her hand, and shook her head. "Connor, whatever your reasons for orchestrating that photo, damage was done. Yeah, I was angry and hurt, but then I saw it as a sign to move on."

How could he expect her to change gears so quickly?

His face turned hard, disbelieving. "You're choosing *Cartwright?*"

"It isn't just that, either. You lied to me."

He rallied, ready to argue the point. "I didn't lie— I. . . ." His face fell as he remembered that night outside Castle Bannon when he'd finally told her about his title. *If you're anything other than completely honest with me from here on out, technicalities or not, I won't even give you the opportunity to explain,* she'd said.

Understanding dawned. For the first time he saw the rift he'd created. It was a fake rift for him, but he'd made it a very real rift for her—whether Wes had come back into her life or not. Connor had been dishonest.

He'd based his entire plan on her emotional immaturity and completely failed to see his own. He needed to push her, to get her to admit the depth of her feelings. The plan, the gamble, had only worked to push her further away.

Because he'd been insecure. Because he couldn't just come back to her, sweep her off her feet, and tell her how mad he was about her. And trust that she felt the same way.

His voice was low, heavy. "Oh, Christ! I just royally fucked this up, didn't I?"

His Irish accent was thicker, the way it always was when he said something especially serious . . . or especially funny, for that matter.

"Lara, talk to me. I'm sorry. I, I didn't mean— I just needed to know how you really felt, to see if it was just a holiday romance to you or something more. It was always something more to me. I needed to know if we were on the same page."

He was so genuine, so naked that she wanted to lean into him. To throw her arms around him. Kiss him. Just be together and let the rest fall away.

But. . . . "You promised to be honest. You broke that promise. I don't know—"

"Would you have admitted the depth of your feelings if I hadn't pushed you?" He cut her off, the anger starting to rise again.

She narrowed her eyes, her fire coming back. "Do you know what I was doing when I saw your little *test* splattered on that tabloid?"

She stood up and started to pace as she remembered.

He swallowed, clearly not wanting to know the answer.

"I was prancing down a London street in Covent Garden, thinking about *how great* it would be to see you." Her voice started to take on a life of its own, and her arms started gesticulating wildly.

"I didn't know when or how since we hadn't talked about it, but it had been almost six weeks. The thought of seeing you again *thrilled* me." She rolled her eyes and shook her head.

"And this is *after* I had just run into Wes and was all happy and feeling twenty-one again. I thought, even if Wes and I picked up where we left off fifteen years ago, there was still Connor."

She looked him straight in the eyes. She lowered her voice and slowed down for the next part. "My beautiful, kind Connor. Who was coming back."

He swallowed, clearly affected by her words.

Her arms came back to life, and her voice rose like one of those wild storytellers at a pub in Ireland. "And then! I stopped at a newsstand to grab a water because I'd just had a bunch of bloody British strawberries—which are still the best by the way; it's like they inject them with serum that makes them all magically delicious—anyway, *the point* is that I was walking down a London street, just counting down the days before I'd get to see you again, and then. . . ?"

She paused, letting the silence get nice and thick with tension. "Can you guess? That's right . . . BAM!" She slapped her hands together. He recoiled like she'd slapped him.

"There are those beautiful blue eyes of yours staring back at me on the cover of some rag and, *oh look*, there's some blonde *supermodel* hanging all over the man I had just been daydreaming about!" She collapsed back into the couch, actually winded from her tirade.

Her body relaxed; she felt better than she had in a week. Letting it all go like that was, on some level, orgasmic.

"Is there no hope, then? Do you want me to leave?" His voice was strained, sad.

"If I asked you to go and leave me alone forever, would you?"

He gulped. The veins in his neck popped, his eyebrows drew together, and his jaw set with tension. A myriad of emotions transformed his face.

"I can't, Lara."

The butterflies started fluttering wildly. Her head started screaming.

Her heart pounded in her ears. "Why not?" She'd intended it to sound stern, but her voice wavered.

His jaw tightened; his eyes searched her face. He was deciding.

Then his voice rose with unfiltered emotion. "Because I love you, woman!"

He shook his head. Frustrated. But his voice softened. "And I'd intended to tell you in a way that was more . . . *grand*. Something befitting you—how amazing I think you are."

His shoulders collapsed forward and his elbows went to his knees. He looked down at his hands. "But I can't hold on to it anymore. It's bigger than me. I love you. I've loved you since you walked into my mother's house and yelled at me for being naked." He chuckled, remembering.

Elizabeth's heart was in her stomach. Her breathing had become shallow. She wanted to touch him. To hold on to him.

Connor stood abruptly, shattering her thoughts. He grabbed his jacket and dropped a card on the coffee table. "I'm at the Ritz."

He leaned down to kiss her on the cheek. Her heart was screaming at her, willing her to bring her arms around his neck and keep him there. Bring him down on her.

But the moment passed too quickly. Her brain didn't have time to catch up.

"I'm not going anywhere," he said over his shoulder as he left the room.

She sat there completely frozen, listening as his footsteps disappeared down the stairs.

The door opened.

The door closed.

And then he was gone.

CHAPTER 15: P.S. I LOVE YOU

Bzzzz. Bzzzz.

Elizabeth threw her arm out, feeling around the comforter, knocking into the box of chocolates she'd brought to bed with her, banging into her laptop which was still open to the Pros and Cons List she'd created, until finally her fingers clasped her phone.

She didn't remember falling asleep, and had forgotten to switch her phone to completely silent.

She hadn't even taken her hair down from the night before.

Bleary-eyed, she swiped the screen until she found the five separate texts.

Lara, I've had to leave for Paris, unexpectedly.

I should be back within the week.

Connor

P.S.

I love you.

Her brain was thick with sleep; it felt like she was still dreaming.

The last two texts reminded her of a movie . . . or they were a movie? Her thoughts went off on a tangent. Which was fine with her because she was still too tired to think about Connor's declarations, or his leaving, or any of it.

She collapsed back, hit her phone's power button until it buzzed in her hand signaling that it was off, and then went right back to sleep.

She spent the rest of her lazy Sunday watching movies and reading and eating more chocolate.

Every once in a while her thoughts would return to what she'd been avoiding.

Connor.

Wes.

Connor, Wes.

The British one showed up at her door that very night.

She'd raced up to her bedroom to make herself decent, only having time to take her crazy hair out of the updo and put it in a ponytail. Mercifully, the curls from the night before held, making it look effortlessly pretty.

She threw on some jeans and a fitted T-shirt and went downstairs to let him in.

Wes had planned a night at Kensington Gardens. There was no breaking in this time. He'd paid a guard and had the Peter Pan statue lit with candles.

He'd also packed a basket filled with white wine, strawberries and Beth's favorite pizza from Pizza Express.

The night was sweet and romantic and thoughtful on so many levels. Her heart was moved, and her head felt the honor of his attentions.

She was overwhelmed by the ease of being with him—her gorgeous Brit, a friend who made the butterflies rise up and who could kiss like a Frenchman.

There were moments when she fooled herself into believing that she'd forgotten all about Connor and his confessions. That the wind had taken her to Wes and that was it.

But Connor's words stayed with her throughout the night, preventing her from giving herself over to being with Wes whole-heartedly.

Whether he sensed her holding back or not, she couldn't tell.

Monday was spent preparing for the show. Audre had Beth come in to take a headshot and to walk her through the rest of the week.

She'd had to write a photographer bio and a blip to go on a white plate next to the display. Audre had given the picture the cheeky title of "Fungie & the Great White" because she said it sounded like a children's story.

She threw her head back and howled with her dark British humor. "Isn't that a laugh? I thought of it instantly! The public is going to love it."

The museum was in an uproar as they prepared the exhibit. They were still printing pieces and configuring the space. Anyone else would have been frazzled, but Audre managed it all with a cool flip of her Carrie Bradshaw hair.

The three girls went out to dinner on Tuesday. Beth filled them in on her weekend.

When Elizabeth described her royal encounter, Audre laughed so hard that the force of it had caused her to literally fall out of her chair.

"What an exciting life you lead," Loryn had said dreamily after she told them about the men.

"Yeah, well, she's catchin' up!" Audre drank the rest of her champagne at the end of the night. She'd barely touched her food, but had gone through several drinks. "From what she's told us, she bloody well stopped livin' and now the Universe is like, "ere, Babes, 'ere you go!'"

Loryn and Beth had burst out laughing as Audre's speech evolved until she sounded more or less exactly like Mel B. from the Spice Girls.

"And naaw, it's rainin' men for dear Liz. And she's stuck between a beeauutiful Englishman and a beeauutiful Irishman." She tipped her glass back to get the last drop of champagne.

Audre shook her head sagely, holding her champagne flute between her thumb and middle finger, while pointing with her index finger. "Someone up there loves you, Babes."

Wednesday was the big judging night. Elizabeth showed up at the museum, more nervous than a valedictorian holding all her unopened college decision letters.

She'd never been the nervous type—not even when she'd tried her first case.

But this. Having her photograph on display? Having others look at it?

Judge it?

It was far more personal—more naked than she'd ever been in public. She'd thought that admitting this vulnerability to Wes just before the ball when she'd looked ill because of Connor's texts was just a cover. Now she felt the truth in it.

It was terrifying . . . and thrilling. The feelings took her back to a time when she'd been fearless. A time when the more something scared her, the more eager she was to do it.

As she walked around and mingled with the other photographers, admiring their work and discussing different techniques for approaching wildlife, lighting and such, she felt like she wasn't just getting acquainted with the photography world, but also re-acquainted with that twenty-one-year-old she'd seen peering out at her from the mirror the night of Wes' ball.

At some point during the night, she'd taken up with Antoine Dupre, a sassy New Yorker with the most beautiful chocolate skin and long lashes. He dressed in typical New Yorker black, but wore red patent shoes and a Lenny Kravitz short defined afro.

He looked her up and down when they shook hands and introduced themselves.

"What I want to know," he shook his head from side to side, "is who did you have to sleep with to become a finalist?"

He pursed his lips together and waited.

She should have been insulted, but it was so odd that she chuckled. "Excuse me?"

"Because, honey cheeekss," he explained, using his hands for further emphasis, "you were not one of the finalists named three months ago. So again, who did your tight little white ass have to sleep with to become a finalist?"

Again she should have been insulted, but his demeanor reminded her so much of one of her friends from college that she chose her instincts over her ego.

With a swag of her head that matched his, she responded, "No one. My work speaks for itself." She crossed her arms for good measure, rising to meet his level of cocky.

"Mmmhmm . . . oooh, you sassy! Dupre likes that." He nodded in approval. "Come, let me show you my masterpiece." He took her by the arm and led her to a large photo of a lion, green-yellow eyes almost straight to the camera. They would have been straight to camera if not for the violet-blue butterfly fluttering just above its head to the right.

It was stunning. He was pleased with her reaction.

"Where's your piece?" he'd asked, now clearly taken with her.

In truth, she hadn't seen it yet. Audre had told her it was in one of the last rooms of the exhibit on the far wall. They walked in that direction, until finally she laid eyes on her photo.

It. Was. Huge.

Audre had blown it up so that it took up the entire wall.

There were a few works blown up in this way so as to take up the space of three pieces—Audre's solution for the photos that had to be pulled at the last minute.

Seeing Fungie that big tugged at her heart. Seeing the great white that large sent the blood straight down to her toes.

Antoine had dropped her arm, his feet involuntarily taking him closer.

"Guurl, you are gonna win—and I'm not even going to hate you for it."

She was still speechless.

"What'you thinkin'? Swimmin' 'round with great whites? Whaat? Oh, heeell no, I don't think so." Antoine had shaken his head and given her a sideways glance that read gurl, you craazay! His New York accent turned Southern in an instant.

When Beth's voice had come back shakily, she'd commented on his photo of a lion and how risky that must have been. It was mostly said under her breath, but he heard her.

"Uh-uh, I was in a glass box, baby cheeks. I am a pro-fess-ional photographer, not some craazay death seeker." He snapped his fingers in the air in a Z and walked off just in time to see a woman wearing an orange dress with dark green boots. "Honey, I know you are not wearin' those shoes with that dress. Come here, let Dupre heelp you. . . ."

Beth stared up, feeling very much the mortal, until Audre instructed everyone to take up their positions next to their photos and wait for the judging panel to come by for the individual presentations.

Beth gave her little speech, more comfortable with the speaking part than the presenting her work part, so she pretended she was talking about someone else's photography, avoiding the word "I" wherever possible.

Newly invigorated by her photographic debut, Beth spent the better part of Thursday and Friday wandering around the city, documenting the lesser-noticed moments of London life.

A woman reading Fifty Shades on the Tube with a smile, a man in his fifties with graying hair and a gray tie giving her a marked look of distaste.

A little boy poking his little finger into the ice cream cone that had just fallen from his hand, now splattered on the cobblestone.

A couple kissing along the Thames with the sunset in the distance.

She escaped behind the lens again and again, avoiding the texts and voice mails that both Connor and Wes had been leaving all week.

She even set a priority ringtone for Barry, the PI, which covered his calls, texts, and emails, so she could feel at ease ignoring her phone completely.

She'd responded to Wes briefly, explaining that she'd been busy preparing for the show on Saturday, but she still didn't know how to respond to Connor.

She kept running into her neighbor, Brian, too. Around the square, at Covent Garden, on Tottenham Court Road. They'd stop to chat here and there, commenting on what a big little city London could be.

Elizabeth passed the time in this way, losing herself in London life and living behind the lens. It was an easy existence, one that she savored, never taking it for granted. She knew that the simplicity of such a life could not last.

Chapter 16: For the Greater Good

By the time Friday night rolled around, Beth had had quite enough of being an observer, going at it alone.

She called Audre first.

"Can't do it, Babes, I'm working. There's still loads to do before the opening gala tomorrow night," Audre had told her quickly before getting off the phone.

Loryn, fresh off of a fight over her husband's dirty clothes, was spending a quiet night in, making up with the owner of said dirty clothes.

She thought about calling Wes, but she didn't want to add to her confusion. She wanted to keep escaping, having fun, interacting with people.

So she made a decision to reenact the night she'd made friends with her favorite Brits.

She chose a small little pub called the Twist & Nob in Bloomsbury. There were about twenty people in the tiny watering hole. Wood paneling everywhere. Nice high booths along the wall on the right.

It was dimly lit, even with the lights hanging from the ceiling at various intervals. The tables and chairs were made of worn wood, like many of the pubs she'd been to in the city.

The place reeked of history. She approved.

It felt a bit shadier than the pub where she'd met her friends, but in a Diagon Alley sort of way.

"Barkeep, a round for everyone on me!" she announced, just like before, feeling how brazen she was being now.

Back then she'd just done it, no real thrill involved. She wanted to do it and so she did.

This time it took some guts.

The people in the pub raised their glasses to her. She nodded appreciatively, grabbing a pint at the empty bar and then making her way around the different groups.

The two older men in the back corner were the most interesting to talk to. Warren and Asher were both in their nineties and had fought in World War II.

Her history degree brain was fascinated by their stories. Harrowing tales of planes being shot down, different women wanting to marry them at various points, losing friends they'd gone to school with.

The two of them had been friends for more than eighty years, and had been frequenting that pub, in its different forms for the better part of fifty years. According to them, there had been eight different pubs located where Twist & Nob stood now.

By the time they had left an hour later, the crowd had thinned to just a handful of people.

She tried to talk to two women who, from what she could tell, were busy gossiping about their friend's marriage and how she didn't know her husband was having an affair.

They hushed when Beth approached. They thanked her politely for the drink, but were clearly happy when she decided to move on so they could continue their shocking stories.

She felt like a third wheel when she'd stopped to talk to a young couple in their twenties who, as it turned out, were only on their third date.

She wasn't sure if she felt like a third wheel because she actually was one or because they were still awkward around each other and she was just the third person to their awkward party.

After a few minutes, she took one of the stools at the bar and nursed her third pint.

The bartender was too busy arranging things behind the bar to pay her much attention.

So she sat there and thought about all the things she was trying to avoid. All the men she was trying not to think about.

Until a rather average-looking man in his thirties ventured into the pub and took the stool next to her.

"Hello," he said cheerfully.

His hair was brown and his features were average, but kind-looking. The type of man you might find in an office that everyone referred to by the name of Bob.

"Hi, there," she said back.

"What brings you out tonight?" he asked.

She took a drink. "Oh, just . . . reliving a memory, I guess."

He ordered a pint and they fell into easy conversation.

She told him about how she'd met her group of friends and briefly about her summer in London.

"How long have you been back in our fair city?"

"Umm, almost a month, I think?"

"And is it everything you remember?"

"More." She nodded.

"Ah, well, cheers to that!" They clinked their glasses together. "I'm Jefford, by the way."

"Beth." They shook hands.

"Soo, is Jefford a common name?" She tried not to be rude, but it sounded so strange to her ears.

He laughed. "Just call me Jeff."

"What do you do, Jeff?"

"Oh, nothing too exciting. I work in an office. Paper supplies."

She hid her knowing smile in her drink.

"What do you do, Beth?"

She gulped. "I'm a—" she started and then realized she hadn't had to answer this question since Mona had asked in Ireland. "I'm a recovering attorney and a. . . ." She wanted to say it, wanted to hear herself say it out loud, but it felt arrogant, conceited somehow, like who was she to claim to be *that*.

But since it scared her, she went for it. "And a professional photographer."

Her face went red, and she took another drink.

She let out a breath, that wasn't so bad. She could be a professional photographer.

Her photo had left Antoine, who was a *pro-fess-ional* photographer, in awe. Audre was a curator and had gone gaga for her work, so maybe she could be. Could evolve from snapshots to professional photography.

She certainly loved it enough to try.

"Is that new?" he observed. "The photography?"

She thought for a moment, "In a way, very new. In another very, very old. I've been taking pictures all my life."

The bartender turned to the handful of remaining patrons, "Folks? I'm just going to pop off to the loo. If you need anything, I'll be right back."

Everyone nodded at him.

"Have you lived in London all your life, Jeff?"

"Mostly." He nodded, his vision distracted by something out the window.

She turned to look at what held his interest, but there was nothing there.

"What was it?" she asked him.

"A black bird was perched on the ledge of the shop across the street."

How odd.

"Huh." She took a drink.

The bartender returned just then and the third-date couple left with a wave. "See ya, Ned!"

"If you'll excuse me, Beth, I think I'll have a visit myself." Jeff checked his watch and walked to the loo at the back of the pub.

She looked over at the two ladies still engrossed in their conversation about their friend Mary, and her cheating bastard husband.

Suddenly, she felt very alone. A strange sort of tipsy surged through her veins as she started to feel the effects of the beer.

Grabbing her clutch, she rummaged through her things to find something in particular. Her fingers grazed a lipstick, another thing that looked like a tube of perfume but wasn't, her cash, hand sanitizer—Jesus, how much crap did she have in there? Finally, she found the phone.

Quickly, she dialed Wes' number. It rang. And rang. And rang. Until she got his voice mail.

"Heeey! It's me, just wanted to say hi. . . . You should come out with me. I'm at the Twist & Nob in Bloomsbury. Yeah . . . I decided to recreate the night I met you and Audre and Loryn, but now there's hardly anyone here. Anyway, just pop on byyy if you feel so inclined."

She sat there for several more minutes, alone at the bar with her drink.

Her nails clicked on the finished wood. Her fingers followed the outline of a heart carving in front of her, over and over.

Jeff was taking a while and with no one to talk to, her thoughts turned to Connor.

All the blood rushed to her face as she stared at the phone in her hand. The way it did when you were a teenager and you were plucking up the courage to call a boy you liked.

Her heart pounded loudly in her ears as she dialed his number. He picked up on the first ring.

"Lara." He sounded relieved she was calling. "How are you?"

"I'm fiine. Just sitting at the bar waiting for my friend Jeff to come back. *How are you?*"

"Erm . . . I'm well." He paused. "Have you been drinking?" He sounded a little amused, a little alarmed.

"Yes, but you know me, I'm fiine." She waved a hand in the air as if he were standing in front of her.

"Yes, I do know you." His voice was steady, pensive.

She could feel the words bubbling up inside her. The way they did when she'd laid into him on Saturday night.

A tiny part of her rational brain cautioned that it was hardly an appropriate conversation to have while sitting at a bar by yourself, but the liquor disagreed with that part.

"Soo . . . what's that about? Saying you love me and then getting up and leeaving? How's a girl supposed to wrap her head around all that, huh?"

When he didn't say anything, she continued. "And then you're like, 'I'm not going anywhere.'" She made her voice deeper, more manly with some pathetic attempt at an Irish accent. "Then by the next morning you're in Paris for the week. 'I love you, see ya' . . . I mean, seriously? Could you be any more of a *contraadicction?*"

Silence.

"Are you still there?" she asked into the phone, temporarily sidelined from her drunk dial.

His voice was strained. "Yes."

"Good." Her voice rose. "Then there's the *I was so in love with you so I went to kiss someone else in Paris so you'd see it in London?* I mean, *duuuude!* What's that about, you know?"

"Elizabeth, where are you?" He was angry.

"I'll tell you where I am. A long way from Paris, that's where." She pressed the red "end" button with some satisfaction.

She set the phone down and slurped the rest of her drink. After a few more minutes of analyzing what she'd said and then wondering why he wasn't calling her back, she picked up the phone.

But Jeff chose that moment to reemerge.

"Yoouu OK?" she asked him.

He looked embarrassed. "Yes, just a bit of an upset stomach, I'm afraid."

She nodded and then turned back to her phone. The numbers were starting to blur.

214

She made a fist with her hand and noticed the weakness in her fingers.

That wasn't right. She'd only had three pints.

She checked in with her body and then suddenly she understood. *When...?* The blood drained from her face as she made a quick mental assessment of what had to be done.

Before it was too late.

The numbers on her phone told her she didn't have much time.

"Hey Jeff, do you want to get out of here?" She smiled brightly.

He smiled back, eager. "Sure."

She collected her clutch and they walked out to the sidewalk.

It was a busy enough street. She hailed a cab on her first try, willing herself to focus and stay aware.

Time was of the essence.

One thing at a time, she repeated over and over. *You can do this.*

She reached out to Jeff, pretending to need help steadying herself, when a man dressed in black sent a right cross squarely into Jeff's jaw.

The force of it almost knocked her off of her feet.

The old street lamp didn't provide much light, leaving Beth squinting into the darkness.

Another car pulled up and a second man got out and immediately took a swing at Jeff.

The cabbie didn't seem to want any part of a street brawl and sped away.

Her eyes adjusted to the dark. The first man was revving to have another go at Jeff's jaw, and the second looked ready to lunge at him from behind.

Everything happened within the span of a few seconds.

She squinted, trying to see exactly what was going on in front of her, until finally she recognized Connor in black and then identified the second man as Wes.

"*What are you doing?*" she moved between Connor and Jeff who was holding on to his face and moaning in pain.

She held up a hand to stop Connor.

And then quickly seized the thing in her clutch that looked like a tube of perfume, but wasn't. She turned to Jeff. "Are you OK?"

"Ye-yes," he stammered.

Her face went from concerned mask to avenger in a second. She stuck him in the ribs with her stun gun. He vibrated in place before he collapsed back to the ground.

She popped the lid back on the tube and threw it into her clutch.

She turned back to the men, throwing her arms out in exasperation. "Ugh. Now I have to get him in a cab and explain it!"

Connor reached for her, palms out, like he was approaching a wild animal. Or a scared child. His voice was gentle, but strangled. "Lara?" He trained his eyes on her.

216

"This man *drugged you.*" He said the last part extra slowly, like she was mentally challenged.

"I know." She was completely calm.

"He *what?!*" Wes wailed from behind them.

"You do?" Connor asked her.

Then he looked in Wes' general direction. "Wait, if you didn't know he'd drugged her, then why did you attack him?"

Wes shrugged. "I saw you have a go." He shook his head. "Seemed like a good idea at the time. Seems even better now." He looked down at Jeff's body and almost kicked him.

Connor shook his head in disgust. He turned to Beth. "Go back to the part where you *knew he drugged you?*"

"Yeesss. *I kneew.*" It came out sounding like *duh, you're so slow.* Her words were becoming more slurred by the second. "That's why I was going to Taaser him *in the car* on our way to Scotland Yard. But now he has to be lifted and everything." She threw up her hands. Their interference had left her irrationally annoyed.

After thriving as a cutthroat attorney, being held at gunpoint, and swimming with great whites, to Beth, Jeff was just some poor sod who crossed the wrong woman.

At most she sounded inconvenienced.

"You knew?" Connor asked again stupidly. Still incapable of understanding what she was saying or what she was doing with him.

She waved an impatient hand at him. She was losing time. "Of coourse, I knew! Do you know how many rape drug

217

hypotheeetical cases you go through in mmmock trial and in laaaw school? A group of us—all women—even drugged each other so that we would know what it feels like and build up a toleranccce."

Wes came to stand next to Connor. They both stared at her like she was an alien from a different planet.

"You knew this man had drugged you, and you proceeded to consciously enter a vehicle with him regardless?" Wes asked.

Ugh. Why were they so slow? She glared at the two men.

Thoroughly disgusted, she explained, "I wasn't going to leeeave this criminal in the bar so he could prey on someone else! Geez. *I'mm fiiine.*"

She swayed where she stood. "Naaw help me get him into 'nother cabbb!"

Connor slipped an arm around her waist to steady her.

Wes dialed a number on his phone, now livid. "I've got a better idea."

"Are you calling the police?" Connor asked him.

Their mutual animosity was tabled for the greater good.

"No, I'm bypassing Whitehall. Phoning MI-5."

Connor looked impressed. "Didn't know they handled such things."

"They don't. I'm owed quite a lot of favors." Wes bent down to rummage through Jeff's pockets. He extracted a vial. "Definitely this piss pot's handiwork."

Wes spoke low into his phone and then put it away. "They'll take care of it so she doesn't have to have anything more to do with this." He was gritting his teeth, hands on his hips.

A minute later a black sedan pulled up. Two men dressed in black picked Jeff up off the sidewalk and then sped away without a word.

Elizabeth's vision was blurring more and more. It was getting harder to stand, even with Connor's help. "I'mm fiiine," she repeated more for her own benefit, but she could hear herself losing control over her speech. "Jusst neeed to get hoome."

"I'll do it." Wes reached for her, attempting to extract her from Connor.

"No, I'll be the one to take her home. Thanks for your help, Cartwright." Connor was both grateful and menacing at the same time.

"Not at all, *Bannon*," Wes said, the iciness returning to his voice. "But I'm the one with the car. And I'll not leave her drugged and unconscious in your care!"

Wes sounded like an indignant knight in shining armor.

"I'm nooot unconsio. . . ." She was fading fast.

"She's perfectly safe with me." Connor narrowed his eyes. "And you've got another thing comin' if you think I'll be leaving her with the likes of you!"

"Hoome. Naau," she managed.

They looked at each other, understanding. Without another word of argument, Connor lifted her in his arms while Wes opened the rear door.

Beth was suddenly sandwiched between the two of them in the backseat as Wes' driver pulled into traffic.

"Jaysus, Lara. You sure do know how to get into trouble." Connor brushed her face with his fingertips.

"How'd yoo fin' me?" she asked him.

His jaw tightened.

She lifted her head up to look at him.

He finally answered through gritted teeth. "I put a GPS tracker on your phone when you left it on the table at Cartwright's event."

She narrowed her eyes, "Wee're goonn tak 'bout tha'." She turned to Wes. "'N' yoo?"

Wes looked from Connor to Beth. "You told me in your message, remember?"

"Ooo, yeea."

And then everything went dark.

Her eyes fluttered open to a pounding headache. She made no attempt to move. Registering the darkness, she tried to orient herself.

She was in her bed. The lights were off.

But there were other people in the room with her.

"Thank you for your concern, but you do not have to stay," Connor whispered to Wes.

From what she could tell, both men were sitting on the small sofa along one of the windows in the master bedroom.

"You are mistaken. I'm *the one* who needs to stay. You really have no business being here. You had your chance, Bannon," Wes whispered back.

And then he continued, "I still maintain that it was highly inappropriate for you to undress her!"

"Well, I wasn't going to let you do it, you eejit!"

Their whispers were getting louder.

Beth brought a hand up to touch her chest. She was in an oversized T-shirt.

"I would have been a gentleman," Wes said.

"I *was* a gentleman about it—besides you've never," his whisper faltered, "you've never . . . you've never . . . *have you?*" Connor sounded unsure now.

"Not that it's any of your concern, but no. Not *yet*."

Beth could literally hear Connor grinning with relief.

"She's going to be awake in a few hours and I don't know how she'll like havin' us here. If neither of us is leaving, then let's at least go downstairs and give her some privacy," Connor said.

"Finally, something we agree on," Wes replied.

Beth saw Wes leave the room. But Connor approached the bed.

She closed her eyes, pretending to be asleep.

He bent down and stroked her cheek with the back of his finger so lightly she wasn't sure he'd done it.

The London Flat

"I love you, Lara," he said, lower than a whisper. She heard him leave, closing the door behind him.

CHAPTER 17: ROYALS & DOLPHINS

"And now, ladies and gentlemen, please join me in welcoming the chair of the judging committee, world-renowned photographer Joseph Sadler," Audre said into the microphone. She and a handful of other people were standing on the small raised platform set in the middle of the largest room housing the exhibit.

The crowd clapped politely.

The room was filled with two to three hundred people all dressed in gowns and glittering jewels.

The gala was everything that Audre had promised. Glitz, glamor, celebrities, royals, and lots of champagne.

Although, Beth was sticking to her *one* glass.

She'd spent the better part of the day recovering from the effects of whatever date-rape drug that repulsive Jeff had slipped into her drink.

It was midday by the time she woke to find notes from Wes and Connor.

Apparently, neither would leave until the other left, which happened sometime around eight in the morning according to their separate accounts.

She was feeling completely recovered now, but that was after a lot of sleep, tons of water, and several green smoothies that helped purify her system.

Next to her, Loryn was dressed in a purple gown that set off her gold hair. She gave Beth a warm smile.

They'd gotten ready together. Beth hired the same women who'd worked on her for Wes' ball. She'd picked a royal blue lace dress, another Reem Acra, although not as extravagant as the one she'd worn the previous Saturday.

They stood listening to the great Joseph Sadler give a summary of the many outstanding entries that were received for the annual Wildlife Photographer of the Year Award. And despite some hiccups—he gave the crowd a knowing look, and the crowd murmured and laughed; apparently, everyone in the art world was in the know—they'd managed to find an extraordinary artist who not only captured a spectacular sight, but a historic one as well.

Beth looked around and gave nods and smiles to the other photographers she'd met on Wednesday, including Antoine, who was dressed in his signature black. He blew her a cheeky kiss.

Her shoulders shook a little as she held back a laugh in return.

The night had been exhilarating. She'd enjoyed walking around anonymously, listening to the museum's most illustrious patrons discuss the photographs.

She felt like a mischievous child as she strolled by her picture casually, picking up bits and pieces of the conversation her photo had sparked.

"It's simply stunning!" "Magnificent!"

Those comments filled her with a giddy sort of glee. A little voice somewhere inside shouted from the rooftops, *They like me, they really like me!*

She laughed at herself a little.

Then there were the other comments. "It's astounding the photographer got out in time!" "Do you think an underwater cage was used? No! There's no mention of a cage. Goodness!" "Oh! It's just so shocking to think . . . who was the photographer? This *Elizabeth* was in the water with that beast!"

These comments forced her to relive those terrifying feelings of mortality that seemed to rise up when she stared at the picture for any length of time. When it took her back to being in the water, to after in the boat, understanding dawning as they watched the monster swim away.

"Elizabeth Lara!"

The crowd erupted in applause.

She hadn't been paying attention. Her eyes found Antoine's first. He was shaking his head, his lips pursed, a resentful but knowing grin on his face.

Loryn touched her shoulder. "Liz, it's you."

She found Audre next, waving at her to approach the stage.

Dazed, she walked to Joseph, who extended his hand. Flashes of light went off in front of her.

"And now, if you'll please join us as we all head to Ms. Lara's piece, where she will regale us with the tale of its creation."

En masse, they walked to the last room in the exhibit.

A small podium had been set to the side of the giant photograph.

Elizabeth stepped up and waited for everyone to squeeze into the room, which was much smaller than where they'd all congregated moments before.

She smiled out at the crowd, slipping into her professional speaker mode, without allowing herself to fully process the weight of what had just happened.

She'd won.

No, no, no. Don't think about that. She forced the thoughts away lest she be moved to start jumping up and down like a ten-year-old.

An act which would likely cause her to fall over in her five-inch heels.

Why were all shoes five inches tall now? That wasn't true; she'd noticed shoes that were *six* inches. To which she'd said, *no.* Just. *No.*

Her feet hurt.

She missed her boots.

She let her thoughts run in this random way as the people filed in.

Wes, Loryn, and Audre were now standing next to each other just off to the right, in the front row.

They were ecstatic for her. Beth smiled brightly at them. She wasn't sure if she was more excited by the fact that she'd won the prestigious award or that she'd reconnected with her friends.

Her eyes kept moving. She was surprised to see Brian there, beaming back at her. She gave him a nod, which he returned.

The last few people took their places in the back. One of them was Connor.

He was giving her his dazzling smile. It was so effective, it made her go weak at the knees.

For a moment, all the noise died down and there were only his sapphire eyes. Only his love. Only the two of them.

She shook her head, snapping herself back to the matter at hand.

"Whenever you're ready, Ms. Lara," Joseph said from her left.

"Yes, thank you." She spoke into the mic.

Elizabeth launched into the story of how *Fungie & the Great White* had come to be.

Explaining how she'd gone for a swim with the playful dolphin and had taken shot after shot of Fungie as he moved in and out of the crepuscular rays that pierced the water.

Elizabeth paused in all the right places and let her voice rise and fall like a true storyteller, painting the picture of what it was like in the water. And how she'd seen a large object in the distance, but was so focused on the dolphin that she hadn't really paid it any attention.

The inflections she'd purposely chosen made the audience laugh.

And then she built the tension when describing how Fungie had suddenly begun swimming wildly around her and put his nose to her feet, forcing her to straighten her legs so he could propel her back to the boat.

Beth took in some of the older women's concerned expressions. Gratified by their looks and little whimpers of displeasure, she knew she was properly building the story.

Her eyes ventured farther back and caught Connor's. He didn't look concerned at all. He looked . . . LIVID. His chest was rising and falling as she neared the end of her story.

Her eyebrows drew together, confused by his reaction, but she kept on faithfully. She described how she'd gotten out of the water and watched Fungie disappear in one direction. And how the large object had turned around as soon as she set foot on the boat.

She chronicled how she and her friend had stood there watching the object swim away and how they'd looked at the back of the camera, zooming in to confirm what their naked eyes were seeing.

"And so, while I'm incredibly honored and excited by this award—thank you to the committee and the Natural History Museum," she nodded respectfully to Joseph and the others standing off to the side, and they bowed in acknowledgment, "I'm just happy to be standing here in front of all you lovely patrons of the arts. Alive. And in one piece." She smiled congenially.

The audience applauded.

"Brava!"

"Well done!"

Her friends chimed in, "Cheers, Elizabeth!"

She stepped down and was immediately surrounded by people wanting to shake her hand and tell her how brilliant they thought she was.

There were dukes and duchesses and lords and ladies. Movie stars and directors—anyone who was anyone in London.

It must have gone on for more than an hour. By the time she was finished schmoozing, her face hurt from all the smiling. She'd gone into automatic pilot at the start of the hour. If she hadn't, she would have formed some insanely high opinion of herself.

It was no wonder celebrities had massive egos. If you kept hearing it over and over and over again, it wouldn't be difficult to become brainwashed into thinking you *were* the best thing to happen to the planet since the printing press.

She approached her friends, who had gathered in the corner. She hugged them all, one at a time.

Wes made sure to hold on to her until she broke away.

"Congratula—"

"No, no. None of that." She waved them off. "I've had quite enough, thank you. And anyway, I was just lucky."

"Just a month back and already starting to sound more British. Welcome back, Babes!" Audre smiled.

"Thank you, Audre." She gave her friend a heartfelt look.

Audre knew Beth well and could read it all in her face. They didn't need to say more.

"All recovered then?" Wes asked.

They hadn't had an opportunity to speak yet.

"Yes, thanks." She smiled, grateful for his help.

Connor approached then. He leaned in to kiss her on the cheek. She gave him a nod and a smile. "You OK there? I thought you were going to keel over during my speech."

"Yes." He smiled, and through gritted teeth, said, "I had no idea the rest of your time in Ireland was so . . . *eventful.*" He chose his words carefully.

"You mean Kil didn't mention it?"

"No, he did not." His jaw tensed reflexively.

And in that moment she was sure Connor had called to yell at him for failing to tell him that both she and Fungie had been in the water with a great white shark.

She turned to the rest of her friends and made all the proper introductions.

It was unclear how things would go when she got to Wes. Surprisingly, they shook hands and exchanged a respectful nod.

Feeling emboldened by her new award, she risked things getting awkward and asked outright, "Why do you guys hate each other again?"

Everyone looked at her with wide eyes. It wasn't the British way. To come out and say what everyone was thinking . . . *in public.*

She shrugged. "What?" They kept on. She waved a hand. "Chalk it up to being a crazy American, if you like, or all this attention going to my head, but someone has to ask. What happened at Cambridge? Was it a girl? Is it an English, Irish thing? Your families have hated each other for centuries?" She looked from one to the other.

"What?"

Connor spoke first. "Emmanuel Brown."

"Uhh . . . OK, you fought over a guy?" She kept looking between them, waiting for an explanation.

"No, over the Tompkins Table," they said in unison.

Audre tried to hide a laugh.

Wes explained, "The night of exams a group of lads from Magdalene got one of our top students at King's wasted out of his mind. Bannon was one of them. Brown failed his exam the next day, which dropped King's ranking to second. Magdalene prevailed that year."

"You eejit! I wasn't a part of that group—which, by the way, included lads from four other colleges; Magdalene was in the minority. I was only there to get Emmanuel home. But you, as usual, jumped to your big git-like conclusions and went all wanker, accusing me in public." Connor's accent wavered between Irish and British the way it sometimes did.

He turned to Beth. "There was bad blood between the two colleges for the rest of that year and the next."

231

She still didn't get it. "So . . . what *exactly* is the Tompkins Table?"

"It's a list," Audre answered, barely containing her giggles. "An academic ranking, the most important one at Cambridge. The different colleges vie for the top spot every year."

Connor finished, "It's like the House Cup in *Harry Potter*, but for academics."

Beth smiled, and then chuckled, and then the laughter started to bubble up. She doubled over in a very unladylike way, bracing herself against her knees as she shook with laughter.

The entire room turned to watch her laugh hysterically. "You . . . fought . . . over . . . a . . . list?" she managed between cackling howls. "Not a girl? Or some big epic drama? I thought *I* was a nerd!"

She slapped her leg and laughed harder.

The way they had addressed each other that first night outside No. 3? She'd thought a blood feud was involved.

Her friends had started to laugh with her—in a more proper British way—but they laughed together happily at the level of insanity required to hold on to a grudge for that long over an academic list.

She ventured a glance up at the men who were, amazingly, smiling at each other.

When she was good and finished, she straightened and smoothed her dress.

In good humor, she looked over her shoulder and announced to her audience, "I'm finished now, folks. Thank you, thank you." She bowed a degree and smiled. Most people laughed; others smiled and looked away politely, continuing with their conversations.

"So, Connor, I know you by reputation of course." Audre looked him up and down like she wanted to mount him. It would have bothered Beth if it was anyone but Audre, who looked at all good-looking men the same way, at some point or another. "Do you have any *flaith* brothers?"

His eyes squinted together as he measured her in return. "Sadly, I'm an only child," he said simply and then gave Beth a sideways glance that showed he was terrified.

She hid her smile.

"Congratulations to you, as well Audre." He gave her a little bow. "This is quite a show you put on every year."

"Thank you. I am but a slave to the arts," she said dramatically. "I understand that you are as well. I'm hearing interesting things about your latest auction house in Paris."

"Yes, it is a work in progress. But I'm hopeful things will come together, just as soon as I can devote more time."

Audre wasn't finished schmoozing him. "Rumor has it that you are trying to get your hands on a rare ruby that has some connection to your family?"

Beth stared daggers at her. If Sade's name came up in this conversation, she and Audre would have words.

Loryn jumped in. "So what keeps you away from your work, Connor? Are you hunting for a special piece in London?"

Connor gave Beth a not-so-subtle look. "She isn't a piece, but she is one-of-a-kind."

Wes straightened.

Connor directed the next comment at him. "Congratulations on your event. It was quite an evening." He nodded courteously.

Wes was surprised by the compliment. "Thank you."

"I'll let you all catch up. I just wanted to give Elizabeth something." He handed her a black box that was roughly the size of her small palm.

He bowed, extending his arm, keeping his eyes fixed on her face. "Miss Lara."

Her heart tugged as she remembered.

She watched him walk away in his beautifully cut dark suit.

"Well . . . are you going to open it?" Loryn squealed.

"Uhh. . . ." She looked at Wes, sensitive to his feelings. And the potential for awkwardness.

Audre turned to Wes. "Why didn't you bring her a gift? That man is *definitely* one-upping you."

Beth's eyes widened.

Audre didn't care. "What? It's what we're all thinking. And what kind of friend would I be if I didn't make that clear to the *both of you.*"

She wanted to wait and open it when she was alone. There was no telling what he'd given her, or the effect it would have.

"Oh, go on then, just open it." Wes threw up his hands, exasperated, but still in good humor.

Audre and Loryn were less encouraging, more *we really want to see and if you don't open it now in front of us we will hound you forever, plus you ditched us for a decade—you owe us.*

She sighed; it would probably be difficult for her to wait anyway. It would linger on her mind until she uncovered the mystery.

She worked it open. Inside was a big shiny crystal, attached to a platinum setting and a platinum necklace. She hooked a finger through and held it up, holding it to the light.

"Oh, never mind, maybe not. That's just a trinket. Not worth anything!" Audre said dismissively, certain that Wes still had a fighting chance.

Something about it was familiar. She held it in her hand, and suddenly she knew.

Her heart stopped. All the noise was sucked out of the room, like a vacuum. She could feel the blood pulsing through her body.

The others noticed.

"What is it, Liz? Isn't it just a bauble?" Loryn asked.

"Yes," Beth nodded. "But it belonged to Connor's mother." The tears came to her eyes. "It's part of a very precious memory of his. One of the only things he has left of her."

She looked up at Wes, eyes shining. Her head tilted, her eyebrows drew together.

He examined her face, reading it, one emotion after the other. Until his face settled too. Resolve. Understanding.

"Go get him, then," he said sadly. He nodded in encouragement, showing her that he really did understand.

Beth reached up and kissed Wes on the cheek. She squeezed his hand before she turned to run after Connor.

CHAPTER 18: THE TRUTH

Elizabeth trotted out of the museum as best she could in her heels, hoping Connor had gone out the main entrance.

She made her way past the throng of people still coming in to see the exhibit. Many called out their congratulations as she passed.

The presentation and her story had been filmed and broadcast to the waiting crowds outside. She waved and thanked them over her shoulder, but all she could think about was getting to Connor before he left.

She stopped to look out past the steps and the barricades outside the main entrance.

He was there, walking down the last set of steps, about to turn the corner.

"Connor!" she called.

The line of people watched as she ungracefully descended the stairs and ran after him. "Connor!"

He stopped mid-walk, his head snapped up. He turned towards her just as she reached him.

"Lara?" He saw her clutching the necklace. "I thought you would wait to open it—"

"Audre, Loryn, they made me do it." She waved a hand, breathless, holding her stomach as she worked to breathe normally.

"And?" His back straightened; the anxiety touched his eyes as he waited for her to steady her breathing. To find out what she was thinking as she clutched his mother's necklace. All he wanted to do was close the distance. To bring her into his arms, but he knew better than to push her in that moment. To touch her without permission. He'd handled it all so terribly.

He hadn't slept well since he first devised his plan in Africa, knowing what a gamble it would be and yet not understanding just how his strategy would affect their future.

He wouldn't give up on her. Couldn't give up. He'd find a way back to her . . . no matter what she said in this moment.

Connor swallowed hard and shoved his hands in the pockets of his dark suit, waiting for Elizabeth to speak.

Beth found her voice as she watched the emotions cross his beautiful face. Excited by the moment and deliciously terrified by what would come next. How it would all change. She searched for the right words, but couldn't wait for her brain to craft some eloquent speech.

Instead, the words tumbled out of Beth in a frustrated pile, "And I love you, you big prat!"

His face cracked into a glorious smile as relief washed over him. "You do." It wasn't a question.

She nodded, returning his smile. Of course, she did. Elizabeth reached up to throw her arms around his neck, finally giving in.

Finally.

Giving.

In.

She closed her eyes as she relished the feeling of him. His smell, his chest, the way his arms closed protectively around her.

It was a relief.

A relief to stop fighting with him. To stop fighting with herself. To just *stop*.

And return his affection.

She wasn't sure how long she'd known. All she knew back in Ireland was that she had her own journey to follow and that had to come first.

It was the right decision, but now she felt the force of the wind and how it had changed.

How it had twisted and turned, but had always meant to lead her to Connor.

He broke away long enough to cradle her face with both hands. He closed the distance inch by inch, asking for permission along the way.

When he hovered above her lips, just out of reach, she propelled herself up on her tiptoes and crushed herself into him.

He moved his hands to her waist and then wrapped them around her, bringing her into him. His tongue parted her lips as he deepened their kiss. He leaned in, bending her backwards with the force of it.

Very Hollywood.

The mass of people waiting in line hooped and hollered. Some whistled, others cheered at their very public display of affection.

Several flashes went off around them, but neither Beth nor Connor cared.

The rags could post whatever they wanted. They were together now, and that was the truth.

He broke the kiss and took her hand, leaving her wanting more.

"Come on, Luv." They walked to the road and hailed a cab. Once inside, Connor didn't let her go. He kept her securely in his lap until they reached No. 3.

They crashed through the door, only making it to the stairs.

Connor cradled her against him so she wouldn't feel discomfort from the steps.

Slowly, he hiked up her blue lace dress, finding her leg and traveling up with just his fingertips.

It had been so long, every touch made her body struggle against the fabric.

His fingers worked their way to her inner thighs and then he found her, massaging her in slow, circular movements.

Her back arched into him, her moan echoed up through the empty house.

His lips went to her neck where he sucked her eagerly, using his strong tongue to leave impressions in her skin.

She used her hands to bring him back to her, kissing him urgently, letting her hunger concentrate in her tongue as it twisted with his.

Eagerly he deepened the kiss, possessing her, until they were so entwined that a low growl escaped his chest.

"Enough of this!" He reached for her. Beth half-stood, expecting him to carry her up the stairs, cradled against his chest.

Instead, he threw her over his shoulder in one brisk move.

He marched up the stairs into her bedroom and threw her down on the bed forcefully.

She looked up into his face. The hunger colored every inch of him, from his eyes to his bulging muscles.

His mouth was slack as he took off his jacket, throwing it to the floor and quickly doing the same with his dress shirt.

When he was bare-chested and down to his pants, she got on her knees and undid his belt, throwing it to the floor with a heavy clack. She undid the top button to his pants before he swatted her hands away and pushed her back onto the bed.

He removed the rest of his clothing and stood at the foot of the bed completely naked.

In all his glory.

Elizabeth's mouth watered as her eyes took in his well-muscled torso, his lean abs, the cut of his V, down to the proof of his desire for her.

Which was long, thick, and perfect.

Her mouth went dry; she fell further into a well of lust. Melted into a pool of desire.

Nothing else mattered but *this* moment.

She needed to be naked. She needed to feel him against her.

Inside of her.

Devouring her.

Possessing her.

He pulled her up onto her knees, finding the zipper to her dress on the side and lowering it, never breaking eye contact.

The hunger, the adoration, the love she saw there was so overwhelming she could get lost in it.

Swim in it forever and never have enough.

He hiked up the dress from below and pulled it over her head, leaving her in her black lace bra and panties.

Her breasts spilled over her bra as her chest rose with each shallow breath.

He brought his hands to her stomach and rubbed them all over her bare skin. Feeling her, reacquainting himself with her. Every touch felt like he was accessing a much more intimate part of her.

Connor put his palm to her breast and squeezed. She took in his strong hand, eagerly wanting more. Her head fell back, and her long hair spilled down her back as she arched into him.

Then he stopped and splayed his fingers in the middle of her chest. She looked up and waited.

He pushed her with his hand, making her fall back again, but this time he came down with her. Pressing his body into the bed, letting her feel him.

She cried out as she felt his need for her press against the thin lace of her panties.

Her hands reached into his hair and brought him down on her, kissing him with her entire body. Hitching her leg up around his hip and thrusting upward.

"Connor, now," she whispered into him, capturing his lower lip and biting down gently.

"Yes, Miss Lara," he whispered back with a wicked grin.

He pushed himself up. She heard the wrapper.

Roughly, he removed her panties and unhooked her bra.

He looked down at her adoringly, possessing every inch of her with his eyes.

Thinking through all the things he wanted to do to her. *Would* do to her.

He grabbed her hips and dragged her to him, forcibly, frantically. Her arms didn't follow her torso, they extended above her as he pulled.

He positioned himself at her entrance.

She mouthed the words "take me," and it was enough to send him over the edge.

He pushed himself into her hard, causing her to cry out with pleasure.

He thrust into her, using her hips to manipulate her further as he flexed and pounded into her flesh.

His tongue went down to her breasts, licking and caressing and sucking her.

Beth moaned like a wild animal, completely out of control. Connor moved his mouth back onto hers to stifle her cries. It had been just as long for him and he wanted to pound her for as long as he could.

Possess her again and again.

He used his organ, moving it inside of her, making her squirm beneath him as she struggled to breathe with his mouth on her.

He was starting to growl into her as his body took over.

He could feel her starting to build, but he wasn't going to have any of that.

They'd been apart for too long; they needed to stay one for as long as possible. *He* needed to be one with her.

In one lithe movement he flipped them over, so she was on top.

She straddled him, their hands interlaced as she used him to steady herself. To rock her hips into him.

The change in position slowed her down. She circled her hips, slowly, deliberately, watching him with her wild eyes. Her possession threatened to unravel him.

She brought both of his hands to her breasts, keeping them there with hers. Letting him squeeze her, massage her as she rode and started the climb.

He could feel it. The tension building.

Abruptly, he lifted her off of him and threw her down on the bed, face down.

Then lifted her again so she was on all fours.

He grabbed her hips and took her from behind, slowing things down. Instead of pounding into her he took her inch by agonizing inch, forcing her to still.

To calm.

She arched her back as he claimed her.

But her moans started to build again, and then she said the word that was his unraveling.

She looked over her shoulder with her beautiful eyes, her long hair swept to one side and she said, "Please," in a breathless whisper.

He wanted to look at her. Flipping her back around one final time, he took her hard and fast.

Letting her build as quickly as she pleased. Letting his weight drive into her as he merged with her completely again and again.

She cried out as she was finally allowed to build towards her release, until she reached the top, and the waves of pleasure rippled through her body. It went on and on. All blinding light. All sensation. Taking her to another time. Another place.

Connor gave in to the urge pulsing through him and cried out her name as he joined her in the light.

Chapter 19: Goodbye to Fantasyland

"Do you know how much I love you?" he asked her.

They were lying naked in each other's arms, Beth's head rested in the crook of Connor's shoulder.

She looked up at him with sated eyes. "Oh, gosh, we aren't going to turn into one of those sappy couples that lie around saying, '*I love you more, no I love you more*' . . . are we?"

"I have lived in this world for two whole months without Elizabeth Lara in my life and I will get as sappy as I damn well please," he scolded.

She laughed.

"God, I love your laugh." His accent was always especially thick in bed.

"I love your eyes. I love your mouth." He brought his thumb to her lower lip, tracing it and then tugging at it gently.

"It's such a relief to say it. I've wanted to say it from the start. I kept trying to show you, let you see it in my eyes. Hoping you would read it in my face. But of course you didn't . . . or *wouldn't*," he corrected, touching a finger to her nose.

"You are one maddening woman, Lara." He smiled down at her. "*My* Lara."

She let the silly schoolgirl smile through as she finally allowed herself to feel everything she wanted to feel for him.

Without judgment.

Without thinking about how long or short it would be.

Without calling it Fantasyland.

It wasn't. It was real.

"Do you know what I've called our relationship almost from the beginning?" she asked him, kissing him quickly and then pulling away, waiting for his answer.

"No, what?"

"I called it Fantasyland, because it couldn't possibly be real." She hid her face in his arm.

"What'd'ya mean, Luv?" His eyebrows drew together.

"This. You. Us. Your castle, your dolphin. It's always felt too good to be real."

"Ah, well, there you have me. You've felt like a dream from the start for me as well. Since I first set eyes on ya, you felt like a home I never knew existed, never knew I needed . . . never knew I could *have*."

He kissed her again before breaking away to continue, "It always felt too good to be true for me as well. Why d'you think I went away and started doubting, questioning whether you felt what I felt about you?"

He'd put his very misguided plan into action because he'd been insecure. He was the one who needed proof that it was real.

She melted into his arms, kissing him with a new urgency, but he pulled away, sitting up.

His face turned serious. "Wait, tell me everything. I want to know about everything that I've missed in your life."

"Ahh. . . ." She was thrown by the change, especially since he looked so delicious in her bed. "Ummm, you want me to start from when we said goodbye?"

He nodded wordlessly.

She launched into her time traveling around Ireland. Telling him about the people and the pubs and the hostels.

About the twenty-something Swedes, the thirty-something Aussies, the forty-something Belgians.

The nights around the fire. The music. The travelers. The talks on life and love and loss.

The bittersweet goodbyes that came after bonding with someone so quickly only to watch them take the next step on their own journey without you. At this she looked at him knowingly.

"It wasn't easy, you know." She brought a finger up to trace his lips. "Letting you go, but it was the right thing for me at the time."

He looked at her sweetly. "I know, Lara." He seized her hand with his, keeping it in place and kissing it. "I just hope that now we can walk our paths together. Because I never want to be without you again."

She bit her lip. "Well, I still have my search for Matthieu," she paused, thinking it through, "but you can come with me."

"Oh, you'll allow it, will you?" His eyes were wicked as he kissed her and then moved his lips to suck on her earlobe, making her giggle and kick out from underneath him.

He knew that drove her crazy.

She pushed away from him, walking out of the room and down the stairs naked.

"Where are you going?" he called.

"You said you wanted to know!"

She grabbed the box of letters and pictures from the living area and then scooped down to pick up the clutch she'd dropped at the foot of the stairs when they'd come crashing through the door.

She came back in, smiling wildly as she registered his hungry expression. He made the blood rise as his eyes devoured her from head to toe.

"None of that." She wagged a finger. "You said you wanted to know."

She filled him in on Mags' letters, the ones he'd missed. Showed him the pictures of her mother. He'd examined those especially carefully.

He looked from the pictures to Beth's face. "You have your mother's nose, her cheekbones, her mouth, but not her eyes." He brought his hand to cradle her face affectionately.

And then she remembered something from the night before. Still leaning into his hand, she said, "Wait, you said you found me last night because you put a GPS tracker on my phone?"

That couldn't be right, *right?* That was the drug.

250

He dropped his hand and fell back. "Ugh. I knew I'd pay for this eventually."

"Wait, *what*?!" she screamed at him, sitting on her knees and crossing her arms. "You *bugged* my phone?!"

That was *so* not OK.

"Not bugged, *bugged*. That would mean I could hear your conversations, or see your calls. No, I did *not* do that." He held out his hands in his defense.

"I simply put a GPS dot on it so I would be able to physically find you."

Something in the pit of her stomach fell. "That's some crazy stalker shit right there." She raised her eyebrows.

Her eyes were wide. "If I ever leave you, are you going to come after me with a knife or boil a bunny in a pot?"

"What?!" His eyebrows drew together. "That's some kind of film reference, isn't it? No! I didn't do it because I was trying to get you back—although, clearly I was. And if I had actually thought about using that as a strategy, I would have. But, no, I did it because . . . because. . . ." He was really struggling.

"Say it!" Beth was impatient for this particular explanation.

"Because that psycho bastard Stephen is out and I didn't want to alarm you. None of us could know what he would do!" He waited, braced for some reaction from her.

Then something clicked with him. "Why don't you look surprised?" he asked.

"Because Bree told me about it the day he got out." Now she was confused.

Connor was trying to keep up. "What? How'd she even get your number?"

"You gave it to Mona, didn't you?" she threw back.

"Well, yes, but only for emergencies. I didn't want you bothered." He looked away, working it out.

"You to Mona to Kilian to Bree." Beth completed the chain for him.

"Jaysus!" He threw an arm over his eyes. "The Irish can be so meddlesome."

"You're telling me!" She removed his arm so she could look at his face. "Wait, how did *you* get my number? Or know where I was staying?"

"Please, Luv." He tilted his head. "I had a PI find out for me once I knew from Mona that you'd settled in the UK."

She thought about that. Surprisingly, it didn't bother her. But the tracker did.

"So you put a GPS tracker on me, *just* because of Stephen?"

He looked at her with a worried expression and something else behind his eyes. "Well, yes, and—"

Barry Lewis' notification bells went off just then, cutting into Connor's explanation, signaling an email.

She held up a finger, ignoring the worried look on his face.

"Lara, there's—"

"Stop!" she demanded.

252

She swiped the screen and found the email. She read it silently first.

Dear Ms. Lara,

I hope this email finds you well. I'll keep this brief as it is rather late and I am quite tired.

I've found Matthieu Fleury in a little village outside Paris. Look for my more detailed email tomorrow.

Knowing how closely you are following this, I wanted you to know right away.

Goodnight,

Barry Lewis

She looked up at Connor. "He's found him!" She reread the email out loud and bounced on the bed with delight.

Everything was coming together, *finally*.

She jumped off the bed and ran into her closet, throwing on some jeans and a T-shirt.

"Where are you going?" Connor watched her from the bed.

"I'm going to pop down to the corner store to pick up some champagne. I'm completely out and I don't want to cut into Sarah's stock even though she encouraged me to," she said in an excited rush, remembering the welcome letter Sarah had sent her from Rome, in the midst of her *Eat, Pray, Love* year.

She sat down on the small couch by the window where Connor and Wes had sat the night before to put on her shoes.

"Because this calls for a celebration!" Her eyes danced as she brought one knee on top of the bed and leaned down to kiss him. "Prestigious photography award," she kissed him, "Matthieu found," another kiss, "gorgeous Irishman in my bed." She lingered on the last kiss.

She got up. "I won't be long." She needed to move, the champagne was just an excuse. Her head was filled to the brim with exciting life events and her skin was buzzing with the electricity of it.

"No, let me go." He pulled at her arm. "It's late; I'll get it. Or we could have it delivered." He moved the sheet off of him.

"Don't be silly, I'm already gone!" she called over her shoulder. "Besides, Bannon, you need to rest up! You owe me a round two, and three and four!" She smiled at him from the top of the stairs.

"Deal," he agreed.

She watched him slump back onto the bed.

Chapter 20: Into the Mystic

Beth turned the corner off of Pembroke Rose, cutting through the alley to get to the main road ahead.

She relished the fresh air moving through her lungs.

The night was chilly for late May. She hugged her arms to her chest; she'd left so quickly she hadn't thought to bring a sweater.

It was eerily quiet for 1:00 a.m. on a Saturday.

Mentally she made a list of the things she wanted to buy. Champagne, chocolate, maybe something salty. . . .

Her stomach growled, a loud protest that made her realize she hadn't eaten since lunch, and even that was only a green smoothie to help get the toxins out of her system. Maybe they should have something delivered, before it got too late. . . .

She was riding some post-coital high, the blood coursing through her brain and body. The thrill of the night's events fogged her senses, or she would have heard the footsteps in the alley with her.

She turned the corner onto the main road and popped into the store. Quickly, she picked out her items, throwing several random things into her basket, just in case they couldn't get delivery. Her stomach roared loudly. Now sufficiently reconnected with her other human urges, she understood that she was actually starving.

In record time, she was on her way again, cutting through the alley and turning back onto Pembroke Rose.

A patch of fog had started to roll into the narrow lane.

As she turned the corner a shadow emerged from behind a tree. She jumped back, almost dropping the champagne. One hand came to her chest, clutching her heart as it raced from the shock.

She squinted at the figure and quickly thought through a course of action. It was late; people were home. She could scream and they would hear. . . .

The figure closed the distance until he stood beneath the light of one of the street lamps opposite Rose Square. He let the light wash over him, so she could see.

It was Brian from No. 4.

"Elizabeth," he said cheerfully.

He wore the suit he'd worn to the gala with a light jacket on top, and a bowler hat that looked new to him.

"Hello, Brian." She exhaled in relief, recognizing him, but still startled.

Brian smiled to himself and looked down before taking another step towards her. "I take it Mr. Lewis has been successful in procuring the whereabouts of Matthieu Fleury?" he asked in a perfectly normal tone, as if they had discussed the subject the entire time.

She'd never mentioned it to him.

Involuntarily, she moved closer. "Who are you?" she asked, thinking through how odd it had been that she kept running into him all over London.

That he had come to her show.

How could he possibly know about the PI? About Matthieu?

"My name is not Brian Lockyear," he continued, just as cheerfully as before. "My name is Brian *Jamison.*"

The name was familiar. Where had she. . . ?

"I," he began, "am the Executor of the Last Will and Testament of Magdalen Lara."

She almost dropped the bag. *Of course.*

She'd left right after the funeral, before all of the legalities could be taken care of. And then she'd thrown her phone into Lough Rhiannon. There was so much left undone with regards to Mags' estate. Somehow all of the legalities had been shoved into the lawyer pile of things she was no longer willing to deal with . . . even though she wasn't the one handling it all.

But why had he taken up residence at No. 4? Gone to the trouble of swapping houses with Olivia? Why had he lied?

"Come." He motioned to her kindly, instructing her to follow him.

He led her to the garden and opened the gate for her. A light misting of fog penetrated Rose Square.

She felt at once at ease with him and wary of what he would bring with him.

Of the possibility that Mags had even more to say beyond the letters.

They sat on the bench in front of the fifty-foot London plane tree. She set the bag down beside her and waited.

"I've known Magdalen for several decades now. We were always great friends, she, my wife, and I. I'll spare you all the boring details you amass when your friendship was as old as ours, but tell you that my wife and I also lost our daughter as a child. So we had that in common with your Mags from the start."

Elizabeth remembered Mags telling her about the Jamisons. From what she could recall, they'd lost their daughter when she was only nine or ten, to leukemia. Later she would find out that Mrs. Jamison had also passed.

"She did mention you to me, Mr. Jamison. Although, I thought it was strange because I'd met most of her friends. I thought perhaps you could be a boyfriend." She smiled at him.

"Call me Brian, please. No, we were always just good friends. The reason we never met was for this very possibility. She'd been very concerned about you for some time. Ever since you started at law school, really.

"She suspected that you might need some guidance to find your way down the line and she wanted you to have nothing to do with the will, so she asked me to serve as executor, even though I'm retired."

"You were an attorney?" she asked.

"Yes, yes I was. That's how I got the house in Sea Cliff." He smiled back at her with bright California teeth.

"That's beside the point, however, she wanted me to be unknown to you in case our methods had to be . . . *creative*."

Elizabeth raised an eyebrow and shook her head. Several thoughts raced through her brain, each needing more answers than the last.

"Don't worry, I'll explain," he continued, seeing all the questions she couldn't yet form.

"It wasn't her plan to keep us apart; it just happened that way, until one night a couple of years ago when we were having drinks on my terrace overlooking the Pacific.

"We were both sitting down, looking out at the sunset, and remembering. Talking about Matthieu, and about my Marjorie, and our kids, when suddenly she turned to me, her eyes crinkled, her look ominous. She said to me, 'Brian, you've never met my Lizzie, have you?' To which I replied that I hadn't. Then she went on, 'Good, I'm glad you haven't. I'm . . . very worried. She hasn't been herself for some time. And I'm getting on in years.'"

Brian turned to her with an amused glint in his eyes. "At that point, I tried to contradict her and tell her that she was as lovely as ever, but she was having none of that. 'Oh, hogwash! Hold your tongue and just listen,' she said to me. 'I think that maybe my Lizzie is going to need some help finding her way again. And if there's one thing I've learned in this marvelous, wretched, beautiful life, it's that tomorrow is never guaranteed for any of us. The time may come when something must be done, and in case I'm not here, I want you to help me with her, OK?'"

He paused there and took a deep breath. The silence of the square surrounded them. A slight breeze picked up and rustled through the trees. The smell of spring and ozone and London filled her nose. She waited.

Brian looked up into the night sky. "She was so serious, I just nodded my acquiescence. We clinked our glasses together and wouldn't speak of that conversation again until she got sick at the end of last year. When she found out that she was running out of time, we put our heads together and divined a plan."

"The letters?" Elizabeth cut in.

"Yes, we thought of the letters. She thought very long and hard about how best to. . . . Forgive me, I don't know how else to say this without it sounding awful. Just remember she loved you very much. . . ."

"Please go on," she encouraged.

"To *manipulate* you, Elizabeth. To push just the right buttons to shake you out of your carefully constructed life. To reconnect you with your past. To who you always were before."

"Before the law?" she finished for him.

Brian nodded.

Beth let out a hard laugh. Mags manipulate her? "That sounds about right," she said to him, remembering how she'd manipulated her as a child, a trait Beth had inherited. "OK, but why did you need to be . . . *unknown* to me, as you put it?"

"Because someone had to follow your progress. Be able to check in on things, *anonymously*. You made that very difficult initially. You left sooner than we had expected. Mags thought you would take a couple of weeks with the letters before you took off.

"We didn't know where you would go, but Mags did suspect Ireland. I had no idea where you disappeared to until you made the tabloids. I was able to track you from there.

"I offered my house to Olivia, your neighbor at No. 4, so that I could keep an eye on things.

"I paid your PI, Mr. Lewis, a handsome sum on the side to keep me informed of his progress with finding Matthieu. He blind-copied me on the email you received a short while ago.

"Mags didn't want you to know what was in the will until you found . . . *certain things* on your way."

She could hear everything he was saying, but she wasn't sure how much of it was actually sticking. "Certain things?" she repeated.

He looked at her seriously. "She sent you on a quest, Elizabeth. A quest to reclaim your life."

He reminded her of some wizard or sage that a person on a quest might find along the way. The fog thickened around them, adding to his mystique.

He continued, "She wanted you to travel, to reconnect with friends, to rediscover your passion for photography. She expected you to leave your beau, *John*, was it? But finding Mr. Bannon was rather unexpected.

"I think, quite rightly I'm sure, that she would have been delighted."

Beth laughed. Tears came to her eyes as she listened to how much time Mags had devoted to correcting Beth's life, when her time was so limited. She had cared more about the next chapter in Beth's life, than the last one in her own.

"The will distributes her property. I won't go into all the small details—I won't insult your intelligence. I can just hand you the document tomorrow. Your reputation precedes you, of course. You're very well-known, even amongst the retired set." He inclined his head and tipped his bowler hat.

She nodded in response, grateful for the compliment, but she didn't yet have words.

"There's money to be sure, not an insignificant amount; several million, in fact. And the house in Berkeley. And. . . ." He hesitated.

"And?" Beth's eyes went wide. She felt the tension he was suddenly radiating, the hesitation.

"And a small château in a village outside of Paris." He exhaled.

"Outside of Paris?" she repeated, understanding dawning almost immediately. To someone else it wouldn't have been enough information to put it all together, but now knowing that Mags had planned it all so carefully, she could see the whole picture. "She knew where Matthieu was the whole time, didn't she?" Elizabeth shook her head in awe and disbelief.

"Part of the quest, my dear." He shrugged.

"That's why she wanted me to find certain things before knowing?"

"Well, yes, she knew you would travel. Hoped you would find your friends again, photography, become that fiery fearless girl she used to tell me about—" His mischievous eyes found hers. "Someday you must recount the story of how you ended up talking about American puritan values on the radio in Sweden." Brian shook his head and smiled.

He looked away from her then and back up at the sky. "But. . . ." His voice was ominous. "There's more."

She wiped a tear from her cheek, unsure of when exactly she'd begun to cry. Her throat felt tight and her skin was hot. "Go on." Her voice cracked.

"Carolina never told Magdalen who your father was, but Mags always had her suspicions. She charged me with an investigation."

Elizabeth stilled. Her heart thumped in her ears.

She didn't wait for him to explain. "Brian, what are you saying?" Her breathing turned shallow. A thrilled sort of panic started to blind her.

Brian turned towards her. With kind eyes and genuine affection, "I'm saying. . . ."

Her heart stopped. Her vision cleared.

"That I've found your father."

A Note From Jules

If you enjoyed *The London Flat* and *The Irish Cottage*, please leave reviews. It can be tough for emerging authors. I spend months pouring my heart into books that I hope will delight and entertain and maybe even inspire. But without reviews, books can fall into obscurity very, very quickly. So please, take a moment and leave a review for each book on Amazon.

Don't be shy, leave your thoughts and help others find me.

♥ With a grateful heart, Jules ♥

Keep reading for an exclusive preview of the *The Paris Apartment* . . . but first here's a preview of the Readers Group Bonus Scene: *Elizabeth & Connor Take a Tour of Hogwarts*. . . .

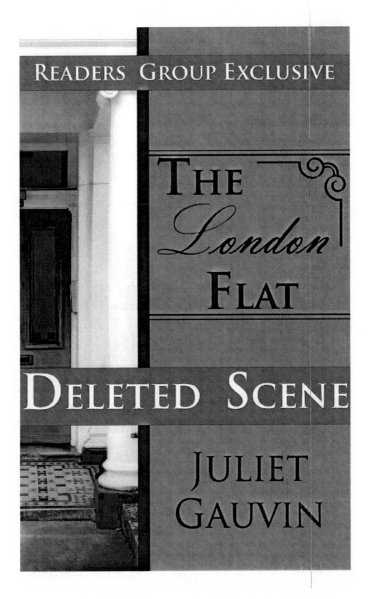

THE
London
FLAT

DELETED SCENE

JULIET
GAUVIN

DELETED/BONUS SCENE PREVIEW: Elizabeth & Connor Take A Tour of the Harry Potter film Studio

The following scene was deleted because it didn't quite fit within the timeline of the book. It takes place sometime after the ending of *The London Flat*, but the scene exists independently from the story (except for the fact that Connor and Elizabeth are now together). This is just a preview, for more join The Readers Group by going to Jules' website: www.julietgauvin.com.

In its entirety it amounts to almost twenty additional pages.

They'd only let go of each other briefly to take showers sometime late that morning. And even then they hadn't been apart for very long, since Connor jumped in twenty minutes into Beth's shower.

She'd been standing there, letting the water hit her neck, her shoulders, and cascade down her back, when the glass door opened.

After so many weeks apart, both of them felt the strong pull to keep within reaching distance of one another. It was less a desire and more a need.

They'd spent the day in bed mostly, only emerging from their love nest long enough to order pizza and for about a half an hour when Beth had insisted Connor come sit with her on the bench in Rose Square.

That evening, Connor procured a car and told her that he had a surprise. She'd looked at him wearily, thinking that no surprise could be better than spending more time curled up next to him on the couch opposite the Chagall or upstairs in bed. But she agreed to go along because the mischievous glint in his blue eyes was so very endearing.

And because he said she could go in jeans and a t-shirt.

The one hour ride through the countryside, passing the green hills and picturesque villages, reminded her how much, on the whole, England reminded her of one long storybook.

Connor held her hand and let her drift off to sleep as the thatched roof cottages started blurring against the rolling green hills and the setting sun.

He roused her some time later when the sky was dark. He'd pulled over to the side of the road and made her put on a blindfold for the last mile. Still drowsy and barely awake, she'd let him.

Five minutes later, the car had come to a full stop, he'd taken her by the hand and lead her across gravel that crunched under her feet, through a set of doors, into a foyer, and then finally through a set of very large doors that creaked with grandeur.

She could tell the doors were large through the blindfold, not just because of the creak, but because the room beyond them must have had a very tall ceiling. Elizabeth could feel a distinct lack of obstruction in the air over her head.

The clack of her boots also echoed slightly against the walls. The room was completely silent except for the sound of their steps. It smelled old, musty, and new at the same time.

"Ready, Lara?" Connor's voice was a low whisper in her ear.

Her lips twitched up involuntarily as he said her name. Their reunion was so new that hearing the adoration in his voice every time he said her name like that, like a caress, still thrilled her.

Saying her name without holding his love for her back, gave him a similar thrill.

Her voice was still thick from her nap, "Yes," she nodded at the same time.

He removed the blindfold, and the familiar twinkling notes of the main Harry Potter theme swelled as her eyes readjusted to her surroundings.

She was standing in the Great Hall at Hogwarts. Long tables set with shining plates and goblets stood ready for Harry and the gang to come marching through the doors.

Beth's hands flew to her mouth. Almost as soon as the music had started and her eyes adjusted to the space, she'd started giggling like a child. After a moment she doubled over and put her hands on her knees, letting her laughter bellow out and fill the Hall.

The London Flat

Join The Readers Group To Read The Rest.
www.julietgauvin.com

THE PARIS APARTMENT PREVIEW

PROLOGUE: FIFTEEN YEARS AGO

"Wes, Mark, wait!" Beth called after them as she and Audre struggled to catch up.

They'd spent the weekend at Cambridge where Wes had been more than happy to play the host. Only Loryn had stayed behind in London.

Beth readjusted her book bag and followed her friends.

"When did you ladies become sloths?!" Wes called over his shoulder as he ran down the hill towards the water. "Let's go, pick up the pace, or we're going to miss the boat!"

"I'm not as tall as you!" she scolded, running after them, now in last place.

Wes had asked one of his friends to take them punting.

Beth had already been punting once that summer when the Yale in London group had traveled to Cambridge to have dinner with the Master of Magdalene, but Wes had prevailed on her regardless; quickly explaining that his friend gave the best tours.

There would be plenty of lurid tales and flasks and swearing. "Everything you love, Liz!" he'd said.

She crossed the bridge, holding onto her bag as it bounced wildly, her things clanging inside.

She looked down over the bridge at the water. They were already inside. She put her head down and really made a run for it, deciding to feel the fun of it instead of worrying about catching up.

She never got to run anymore; even running to class was really a fast walk or jog. She was by no means a runner, but she missed *running*.

Running across a great big green lawn. Running down a hill. Running into the ocean. She resolved right then and there that she would do more of it.

She laughed as her pony tail fell to her shoulders and then fell completely. Her hair blew wildly in the wind, billowing out behind her. She'd just reached the edge, rounding the bridge and turning towards the water when she smacked into someone.

Hard.

She fell backwards, but the person she'd run into flung his arms out and caught her before she fell to the ground. In one quick move he placed her upright again.

He bent down to pick up her bag, shaking his wild light brown hair out of his face.

She looked gratefully into his blue eyes, made electric by the sun. "Thanks and sorry!" she said taking the bag from him.

Their fingers grazed each other in the exchange. It was a typical British summer, hot and humid, but a chill ran down her spine.

"Let's go!" Audre and Wes called together, bringing her attention back to the water.

She looked over at them gesturing impatiently from the boat.

"Well, see ya!" she smiled up into the handsome face of the man she'd just collided with.

He watched her go. "What's your name?" he called.

She half turned, with a mischievous smile she answered, "Just call me Fate!" She winked at him.

And then she got in the boat and drifted away.

. . .

More From The Paris Apartment

Beth opened her eyes to the cold, damp, darkness.

Her vision was blurred.

Instinctively she brought a hand to her head.

She blinked trying to focus.

Her other hand felt the ground. Her fingernails dug into the cold, damp, dirt.

Her eyes couldn't focus on anything and then she realized why.

There wasn't enough light. The only light was coming from behind her. It was just enough to make out the hole of the cave.

She tried to remember how she'd gotten there, but she heard the footsteps approach. She resumed her position on the ground, not wanting her kidnapper to know she'd regained consciousness.

A flashlight shone in her face.

Don't squint Beth, don't move a muscle.

The light passed over her body and then she heard the footsteps retreat.

She looked up to see the person disappearing just beyond the hole.

The cave was musty. It smelled of old earth.

Beth sat up, tuning into her senses.

She could hear water dripping from somewhere nearby. And something else moving. Bats maybe?

She focused on her sense of hearing, trying to push out beyond the cave.

There was nothing. No road. No cars. No people.

She wasn't in one of the well-known series of caves often frequented by the tourists.

Think Beth. Think!

How had this happened? How long had she been gone?

She was just in bed with Connor that morning. Or was it yesterday? *Shit!* She had no sense of how much time she'd lost.

Wasn't there a party? She remembered being at Château Fleury.

Her stomach growled, but she didn't need to go to the bathroom. What did that mean?

When was her last meal?

Her head started pounding, or rather she reconnected with her pounding head. She used her fingers to check her skull for bumps and gashes.

There was nothing.

She'd been drugged then? She remembered looking up at the stars and then it all went blank. It had to have been the champagne—and it had to have been something very strong to knock her out so quickly.

Connor, Matthieu, and Brian must have people out looking for her by now.

The whole village maybe.

What did these people . . . or person want?

The questions flooded her brain, causing the pain to shoot through her temples like a needle. She pressed both palms to her head and squeezed, making a vice.

She went through her pockets, checking for her phone. Taking stock of everything she had on her.

There was nothing. They must have taken it all. Whoever *they* were.

She had nothing on her except the clothes on her back, her shoes . . . and the ring on her finger.

ACKNOWLEDGEMENTS

This book would not have been possible without the support, inspiration, and moxie of the YWLA Writers Group.

Thanks also to the random Starbucks manager in Florida who sold me all the back supply of the now discontinued Starbucks Tazo Earl Grey tea sachets on eBay.

Finally, thanks to all of my friends around the world—even the ones I haven't met yet. You all continue to inspire.

ABOUT THE AUTHOR

Juliet is originally from California. She is a true, hopeless, all-in romantic. Her first kiss was with a Frenchman in Paris, her first love was an Eagle Scout, and her first crash-and-burn was with someone from Harvard (Jules studied history at Yale—she should have known better). When she isn't writing she can be found photographing landscapes, binge-watching entire series on Netflix, or dancing the international cha-cha.

The London Flat was inspired by her time living in London. She loves the Irish, but she loves the Brits as well. Her dream isn't a house on Maui, although she would be perfectly accepting of such a gift from the Universe; her dream is a London flat, and maybe one in Dublin, and one in Edinburgh. =P Can you guess where her next series might be set?

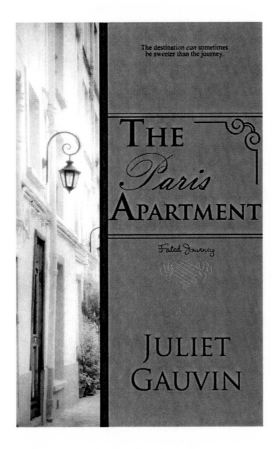

CPSIA information can be obtained
at www.ICGtesting.com
Printed in the USA
LVOW11s0859050617
536961LV00002BA/168/P